LOVE LIKE THEIRS

(THE ROMANCE CHRONICLES—BOOK 4)

SOPHIE LOVE

CHAPTER ONE

Keira opened one eye. As her mind transitioned from sleep to consciousness, it dawned on her where she was. Bryn's couch. Again. Just like yesterday and the day before and the day before that.

She groaned, squeezing her eyes shut again, willing herself to go back to sleep. When she was asleep all that stuff with Cristiano disappeared. She could pretend she'd never broken his heart, that she'd never walked away from possibly the best love of her life. In her dreams, she could also pretend she'd sorted herself out, that she wasn't still sleeping on Bryn's couch, wasting her days watching reality TV, avoiding all her friends' calls, and constantly delaying her boss Elliot's request for her to choose a location for her next overseas assignment.

The room was dark in the weak early December light. As she lay on the couch, staring up at the shadows on the ceiling, Keira became aware of the sound of running water. The shower. Bryn must already be awake, which was unusual considering it was a Saturday morning and Bryn had been hungover every Saturday morning of her adult life.

Confused, Keira sat up, the old couch creaking beneath her, and heard the gurgle of the coffee machine. She sniffed and the aroma filled her nostrils. Bryn was up *and* making coffee? That wasn't like her sister at all! Something was up. Bryn was the slob of the pair, but these days it was Keira who lay around all day getting nothing done. But she couldn't help it. After everything that had happened with Cristiano, she just wasn't ready to face the world.

Keira heard the click of the bathroom lock, then the sound of Bryn's heavy footsteps as she bounded down the corridor. Keira could hear her whistling a toneless tune. She came into view, wrapped in a yellow towel, with another wrapped around her head.

"Oh, you're awake," Bryn said, stopping in her tracks and smiling broadly. "I made coffee. Want some?"

Keira frowned suspiciously. "Why are you in such a good mood? It's Saturday morning. Come to mention it, why are you even up?"

1

Bryn laughed. "I had a quiet night in. Turns out when your liver isn't busy trying to filter poison out of your body, you feel kinda good."

"I've been trying to tell you that for years," Keira mumbled. She sunk back onto the couch, resuming her position looking up at the ceiling. A second later, Bryn's face appeared over her. Water dripped from stray tendrils of hair onto Keira's face.

"You do a very convincing impression of a corpse," Bryn told her.

Keira scoffed and folded her arms across her chest, looking away from her sister.

"That's even better!" Bryn joked.

Keira just ignored her. She heard Bryn move away, heading back to her bedroom to get ready for the day. Keira felt bad for being so snappy with her sister, especially considering the huge favor Bryn was doing her by allowing her to live in her apartment rent free. But then she remembered the myriad times Bryn had been snappy and ungrateful with her and decided that a little bit of role reversal wasn't so bad.

She heard Bryn pad back into the living area. "I'm pouring you coffee," she announced.

Keira sighed and sat up. "I don't want coffee," she said. "I don't want anything that will interrupt my sleep. I just want to sleep forever."

She looked over as Bryn ignored her request, pouring her a coffee into the biggest mug in the house. She came over and handed it to Keira.

"I'm not letting you waste another day on that couch watching Netflix and feeling sorry for yourself," she said, handing her the cup. "Drink this. Wake up. When was the last time you showered?"

Keira frowned as she took the steaming mug. "Thursday evening."

Bryn rolled her eyes. She whirled back to the kitchen counter and poured herself a mug.

"Why are you up so early anyway?" Keira muttered, taking a little sip of the coffee. It was scalding hot. She placed it down on the side table.

"Because..." Bryn sung, reaching onto her tiptoes to fetch a new bottle of her favorite caramel syrup. "Felix and I have plans." She landed back on her heels, syrup in hand, and grinned at Keira triumphantly.

Felix. Felix. Felix. That was all Bryn ever talked about these days. She'd gone from being a serial man-eater to a committed girlfriend. In any usual circumstances, Keira would have been thrilled for her sister finally settling into a steady relationship, but Felix was the same age as their *mother* and Keira couldn't help getting a bit creeped out. It felt a bit too Daddy-Issues for her liking. The fact their own father had abandoned them when they were infants only added credence to her theory.

"What kind of plans?" Keira asked.

She saw a distinct blush creep up Bryn's neck. She shrugged in what Keira instantly recognized as an attempt to look nonchalant. "Oh, just a bit of home decor shopping."

Keira narrowed her eyes. Why would that be making Bryn blush? Perhaps because it was the kind of thing an *adult* did, and that was something Bryn, much like Peter Pan, had sworn against ever becoming. Or perhaps because her party-loving sister was embarrassed to admit she could have as much fun choosing lamps with her lover as she once did raving all night in a New York City nightclub. Or…

"When you say home decor you don't mean an ornamental cat for the mantel, do you?" Keira asked, swiveling to get a better look at Bryn's face.

"No," Bryn replied in her same sing-songy voice. "I mean more like furniture."

Keira gasped. "Why are you picking out furniture with Felix?"

Bryn instantly flushed a deeper shade of red. "He has a new apartment, that's all. It doesn't *mean* anything. Stop looking at me like that!"

"Are you moving in with him?" Keira demanded, firing another quick question at her floundering sister.

"I don't know," Bryn laughed. "Who knows?" She buried her head in her coffee mug, attempting to hide her grin with it but failing miserably. There wasn't a coffee cup in the world wide enough to conceal the wideness of Bryn's smile.

Keira was stunned. She couldn't believe what she was hearing. Her sister had finally been tamed. The drama was worthy of one of her articles!

"Anyway, stop trying to change the subject," Bryn said, suddenly. "We were talking about *you* and how you're turning into a couch potato. You can't spend another weekend at home. Please, get out and do something. It's really not good for you to sit around inside all day."

"It's cold out," Keira moaned.

"So?" Bryn replied. "Wear a hat! You're born and bred New York City, you can handle the cold!"

3

Keira chewed her lip. She remembered a text that had come through from Shelby last night. She hadn't responded yet, but her friend had invited her to a party Saturday evening, which was tonight.

"Actually, I'm going out this evening," Keira told Bryn, sounding smug.

"You are?" Bryn asked, arching an eyebrow in obvious disbelief.

"Yes," Keira replied bluntly. "I'm going to a party. I was going to ask you to come along."

"I'm glad to hear it. But I can't. Felix and I are having an early night."

Keira laughed loudly. "Who are you?"

Bryn laughed. With a little shrug she said, "People change."

When Keira gave little more than a grunt in response, Bryn sat down beside her and rubbed her back. It was very unusual for Bryn to be so caring.

"I know you're hurting," she said in a soothing, maternal voice. "But dwelling on the pain does not help you heal. You need to get up and face the day. A shower would be good for you."

"Fine," Keira grumbled. "I can take the hint."

She got up from the couch, her muscles aching as she did. The crick in her neck was becoming a permanent feature now.

"I'll be gone by the time you're done," Bryn said.

"Okay, have a nice time," Keira replied. "Send my hellos to Felix."

Bryn blushed immediately.

Keira went into the bathroom, shaking her head at the complete transformation of Bryn. It was amazing how much the love of a man had changed her sister, she thought, as she peeled off her grubby pajamas and turned on the water. She stepped inside the cubicle, closing it behind her.

As the water ran over her hair and skin, Keira marveled at the role reversal she and Bryn were going through. As much as Bryn had changed for the better, Keira felt that she herself had changed for the worst. The end of her relationship with Cristiano had hit her like a freight train. It was even affecting her work. Elliot was eager to send her abroad again for another assignment, but they'd had three meetings about it now and each time Keira had found an excuse not to commit to a location. When he pushed, she'd remind him of how he'd promised her more creative freedom after the last assignment, and that would shut him up temporarily. But it couldn't last forever, she knew that. Just like how living in Bryn's apartment

4

and sleeping on her couch couldn't. Keira would have to pull herself together sooner or later.

She washed the lather from her hair, realizing as she did so that Bryn had been right. A shower was just what she needed to rejuvenate her mind. Perhaps going to a party this evening would be good for her, even if she didn't feel like it. Sometimes what you want and what you need are different things, Keira reminded herself. Those words had become her personal catch phrase whenever she found herself beating herself up over what happened with Cristiano. Just because she'd wanted him, didn't mean he was right for her. Still, sometimes it was easier to believe her own words than those of others.

She stepped out of the shower, wrapping herself up in fresh towels, and went back to the living room to find some clean clothes for the day. All her stuff was still in boxes and suitcases, but she'd become so accustomed to this way of life now she knew where to find most things. The top she was after would be in the shoe box under the coffee table. She crouched down to reach it. As she did, her gaze fell to her cell phone. She fought the familiar compulsion to check and see whether Cristiano had been in touch, instead grabbing the box and rummaging through it for the top she wanted. As she pulled it out, she remembered the last time she'd worn it: Paris, during one of their romantic strolls through the rain-soaked city. Her heart ached immediately, and she dropped the top, grasping instead for her phone, her willpower suddenly gone.

She had no notifications but checked every app individually just in case he'd decided to get in touch through some slightly more obtuse means than text or email; a "like" on one of her photos, for example, or posting a link to a relevant news story on her wall. But with a sad sigh, Keira realized there was nothing. Cristiano had made no attempt to reach out to her, even subtly, since she'd ended things in Charles de Gaulle Airport.

The uncomfortable sensation in Keira's chest made her realize how much she needed to see her friends tonight. A party might not be the best environment for her right now, but being with Maxine and Shelby would be. For the first time in a long time, she found herself looking forward to human company.

*

Keira hurried up the steps of Shelby and David's house. It was freezing, and she was dressed in a barely there black dress. She shivered on the step as she pressed the bell over and over, impatient for the door to be opened.

At last it swung open, letting light, music, and chatter pour out at Keira. She rubbed her arms and looked up to see Rob, David's brother, at the door.

"Hey," he said, looking her up and down. Then an amused frown appeared between his eyebrows. "Keira Swanson? Is that really you?"

"Yup," Keira replied. "Can I come in? I'm freezing!"

"Of course!" Rob replied, moving out of the way. Keira hurried past him, out of the darkness and into the brightly lit corridor. He closed the door behind her. "I didn't recognize you. You've changed."

"I'm not twenty-one anymore, if that's what you mean," Keira replied, shirking off her jacket.

Rob took it from her, hanging it on a spare peg. "Was that the last time I saw you?"

Keira nodded. "Yup. Graduation from college." The heat from the apartment began to warm her and she stopped rubbing her arms quite so vigorously. "So, how are you?" she asked Rob, attempting to make polite small talk.

"I'm great," he replied, beaming. "Yeah. All good." He scratched his head, looking lost for words. "Um, why don't you come in?"

"Sure," Keira replied.

He gestured for her to go further inside the apartment. Keira did, following the noises toward the kitchen. David and Shelby had a nice house, considering no one else Keira's age had been able to afford to buy their own home yet. Hell, Keira couldn't even get together the money for a deposit on an apartment to *rent*!

She found everyone in the kitchen, Shelby perching beside the large kitchen island chatting with some people Keira didn't know. Work colleagues, she presumed. They looked pretty put together, with neat hair, trendy outfits, and confident smiles. Keira felt suddenly very uncomfortable in the presence of these apparently calm, collected other friends of Shelby's.

"Keira!" Shelby exclaimed, noticing her then. "You came!" She placed her glass heavily onto the counter and wobbled toward her friend, clearly already a little tipsy. "Oh my God, I never thought I'd see you again," she wailed, throwing her arms around Keira's neck and squeezing.

Keira patted the arm that choked her. "Don't be silly," she squeaked. "I've just been taking a bit of off time."

Shelby moved out of the vise-like embrace and looked her up and down. "Wow, you look gorgeous!" She plucked the fabric of Keira's dress in her fingertips, making it spring back against Keira's hips. Then she turned her head to address the room. "Look how gorgeous my friend Keira is!" she cried. "AND she's SINGLE!"

Keira blushed immediately. "Please, Shelby," she muttered out the corner of her mouth. She felt less than attractive, no thanks to the extra pounds she'd gained recently.

"What?" Shelby giggled. "You're back on the market and I have some very handsome friends. And girl, your ass is looking fine."

"There's a difference between fine and fat," Keira muttered. "And I'm not ready to date yet. This is literally my first evening out of Mope Mood in two weeks."

"Okay, okay," Shelby replied, rolling her eyes. "I won't push it. But I will give you some wine." She grinned devilishly.

"No!" Keira protested. She knew far too well what a sloppy drunk she could be, and how easily she drank too much when she was feeling emotional. Alcohol was the last thing she needed right now.

But it was too late. An overfilled glass of white wine was thrust through the crowd toward her. She took it from the extended, bodyless hand, peering through the crack between people's heads to see who was offering it.

"MAX!" Keira cried, when she realized, finally, it was her other best friend.

Max wedged herself through a small gap between two tall, immovable-looking guys, and hugged Keira.

"Hi, stranger," she said. "It's so good to see you." They drew apart and Maxine smiled at her, her dark eyes glittering with kindness. "I was so worried about you I even texted your sister."

Keira's eyebrows shot up. Maxine and Bryn hated each other. Some inexplicable feud neither could remember the origins of made their relationship frosty at best.

"She didn't tell me," Keira said.

"Of course she didn't," Maxine replied, rolling her eyes. "Anyway, I'm glad you're here now. Now I can tell you face to face that you're a strong, powerful, wonderful woman who's not defined by a man."

Keira laughed. It felt like the first genuine smile she'd cracked in days.

"Thanks, Max," she said, nudging her friend.

Feeling a little happier, Keira took a sip of the wine. It was nice, with a delicate, light flavor. Instantly she could imagine Cristiano's voice in her head, telling her it would pair wonderfully with seafood. She felt a pang of loss.

"Have you noticed that Rob is staring at you?" Maxine asked suddenly, breaking into her thoughts.

"No," Keira said, looking over to where he was leaning against the fridge. He looked away immediately.

"You should talk to him," Maxine urged. "He clearly likes you."

Keira shook her head. "I'm not in the right place to be *liked* right now. Cristiano was a rebound from Shane, remember. And look how badly that went."

"Shane was a rebound from Zach," Maxine reminded her. "And it was the best decision you'd made for yourself in a long time."

Keira shook her head again. She lowered her voice. "Please can I just have one night without thinking about relationships?"

Maxine let out a reluctant sigh. "Fine. But on one condition." She grabbed Keira's hand. "You dance with me all night!"

Keira exhaled loudly but didn't put up much resistance as Maxine tugged her into the middle of the living room. The couches had been pushed back, the coffee table moved to the side, and there were a few other people already dancing in the space. Standing right in the middle of the room like that certainly wasn't Keira's first idea of fun, but anything was better than being forced into flirting.

Shelby bounded over then, throwing her arms around both Keira and Maxine.

"My faves!" she cried. "Have I told you two recently how much I love you?"

Keira laughed.

"Someone's drunk," Maxine commented.

"Yup!" Shelby confirmed. Then she raised her voice and yelled over the music. "And it feels awesome!"

They began dancing together to the track, pulling silly, overly enthusiastic dance moves. Keira let herself relax into the moment. She drank more from her glass of wine, giving herself permission to enjoy herself and let her hair down just a little bit. With her best girlfriends she could loosen the reins a bit.

Her glass was empty when Shelby suddenly exclaimed loudly, "Oh my God! When was the last time we did shots together?"

She grabbed both their hands, looking from one to the other with expectant excitement, like she'd had the best idea in the world.

"No way," Keira said, shaking her head. She was already one extremely large glass of wine down. Adding a shot to the mix would be dangerous.

"Come on!" Shelby said, pouting. She bounced up and down, her expression and tiny frame making her look like a petulant pixie. "We have tequila!"

Keira recalled how the three of them had always had tequila shots back at college parties, almost ritualistically on a night out, and just how much fun it had been.

"For old times' sake?" Maxine said, nudging her.

Maybe one wouldn't hurt, Keira thought.

"Okay, okay," she said finally, giving in to peer pressure for the umpteenth time that night.

Taking Keira by the shoulders, Shelby steered her over to the kitchen counter, Maxine following behind like a conga line. David was there talking to a group of his male friends, Rob included.

"Babe, we're doing tequila," Shelby slurred, reaching an arm around his shoulders and planting a sloppy kiss on his cheek. Her engagement ring sparkled under the bright lights.

David gave her one of his adoring looks and Keira looked away, feeling a pang of jealousy deep in the pit of her stomach. As she averted her gaze, she inadvertently looked straight into Rob's. He seemed to have a matching expression to her own, like he was holding back envy. She wondered whether he was currently riding the wave of a breakup like she was.

"Of course, my darling," David told Shelby, kissing her nose.

She unslung her arms from around his neck, and he went over to the cupboards, collecting the things they'd need—tequila bottle, salt, and shot glasses.

"Rob, can you get the limes?" Shelby instructed, pointing at the fridge his back was against.

Keira watched him fish a bag of limes out from inside the refrigerator. He came over to the counter and placed them down.

"I'll have one of those, too," he said, nodding to the row of shot glasses David was lining up.

"HELL YEAH!" Shelby cried.

She reached for a knife to begin cutting limes and promptly had it removed from her hand by Maxine.

"Let me do that, okay, hon?" Max said with a giggle.

Shelby nodded.

Once everything was ready and the shot glasses filled, David, Rob, Keira, Maxine, and Shelby took their positions in front of them. They salted their hands and each picked up a shot glass, readying themselves for the countdown.

"Three, two, one!" Shelby cried.

Keira necked the shot back. The liquor burned her throat immediately. The taste was intense and she swallowed quickly, feeling heat race down her gullet. Wincing, she licked the salt quickly, then grabbed a lime wedge and sucked on it.

With watering eyes, she looked over at her friends. Shelby pulled her own lime out of her mouth and threw it onto the countertop, before suddenly retching. Then she turned and threw up violently in the sink.

David burst out laughing, and hurried over to comfort her. Maxine followed suit, discarding her lime and giggling loudly.

Keira was left just with Rob. She looked over at him. He was laughing, his lime still wedged in his mouth.

"Shelby is such a lightweight," he said, taking it out finally.

Keira took her own lime out of her mouth. The tequila reached her stomach, and warmth spread all through her.

"It's not her fault," she said, smiling. "There aren't many five-foot-nothing, hundred-pound women who can hold their liquor."

"You're doing okay," he commented.

Keira patted her newly rounded stomach as if it were an explanation.

"So, anyway," she said. "What did you think of your shot?"

"It was all right," Rob replied, shrugging nonchalantly. "But I've gotta admit, I'm more of a beer guy. Thought I'd give it a try."

"I commend you," Keira replied.

She could feel her cheeks getting warm from the mixture of wine and liquor. For the first time in days, she felt willing and able to have a conversation.

"So Rob, what have you been up to for the last..." She counted in her head. "...seven years?"

"Regenerating every cell in my body," he said.

Keira frowned with confusion. "Huh?"

"Seven years. That's how long it takes for every cell in your body to have regenerated," he explained. "There's a theory that it's why people get a seven-year itch in relationships."

"Oh," Keira said. "I don't think I'll ever reach seven years in a relationship."

Rob laughed. "No. Me neither. I can do one. Sometimes two. But anything beyond that is unknown territory."

"Same," Keira replied. She could tell the alcohol had already loosened her tongue somewhat. It felt nice to enjoy communicating again. She reached for the tequila. "Another?"

Rob raised his eyebrows. "Sure."

Keira poured them each another shot. They took it in turn to salt their hands, and then this time, she counted them in. "Three, two, one!"

They took the shot in unison, slamming their glasses down at the same time, licking their salted hands and reaching for the lime slices. They both went for the same piece, and Keira playfully batted Rob's hand away, snatching it up from him. She sucked it, laughing, then took it from her lips.

"That was funn—" she began, but her words were cut off when Rob suddenly lunged in and kissed her. Keira pushed him away, horrified. "HEY!" she shouted. "What the hell was that?"

Rob looked stunned. "What do you mean?" he demanded. "You were flirting with me."

"NO I wasn't!" Keira said back. Worse than having someone's lips on hers without consent was the accusation that she'd given him some kind of green light to do it when she most definitely hadn't.

"Oh, please," Rob replied, looking incensed. "Why did you keep looking at me then? Why did you offer me another drink?"

"Since when was looking akin to flirting?" Keira replied.

"Um, ever since our species evolved distinct male and female parts?" Rob shot back.

He looked furious. Keira realized then that he was actually inebriated. He'd been holding it well before, but with those two shots of tequila in quick succession, he'd clearly crossed over the line of what his body could handle, and he was suddenly looking very disheveled.

Keira turned away, not prepared to have a discussion with a drunken idiot over the nuances of flirting. But as she walked away she was stunned by Rob grabbing her arm, attempting to hold her back.

"Hey," he said. "You should apologize."

"What?" she demanded, the tequila swilling in her stomach giving her confidence. "YOU should apologize. I haven't done anything."

"You led me on!"

Keira felt rage take over. "You're a pig!" she cried out, reaching for the closest glass of alcohol. She found a discarded, full wine glass and threw its contents into Rob's face.

11

She hurried away, grabbing her coat and scurrying from the house before anyone had a chance to stop her. She didn't want Maxine or Shelby tailing her, trying to comfort her. She just wanted to go home.

Luckily, as she rushed down the street, a cab was coming her way, its light on. She hailed it.

It slowed at the curb and she leapt inside, telling the driver Bryn's address. As she sped away, she saw Maxine and Shelby hurrying onto the doorstep, looking for her. She waved meekly at them from the back of the cab as it passed, then hunkered down in her seat. Humiliation made her cheeks burn. She rummaged in her purse, grabbing her cell phone to text Shelby an apology. But instead of messaging her friend, she found herself sending a message to Cristiano instead. Three simple words.

I miss you.

CHAPTER TWO

When Keira woke the next day, a feeling of mortification struck her. Memories of the party came flooding back, of the tequila shots with her friends and the whole unpleasant experience with Rob kissing her, and her throwing a drink in his face. But that wasn't the worst thing. The worst thing that had happened was that she'd texted Cristiano.

She heaved back the covers, getting tangled in them in her haste to find her cell phone and falling flat on her ass. From the hard floor, she groaned and reached up to the coffee table, getting hold of it.

Once the phone was in her hands, Keira became too terrified to look. She hesitated, her thumb hovering over the button, before finally swallowing her anguish and pressing down.

Immediately, she saw she'd received several text notifications. Her heart leapt into her throat. Could one be from Cristiano? She clicked on the icon.

The first was Maxine asking if she was okay. The next; Maxine, again, asking her to let her know she got home okay. Then several from Shelby writing a stream of unconnected words spelled incorrectly, another from Maxine from earlier this morning stating that if Keira didn't get in touch by midday she'd call the police, and finally one from her mom asking if she'd ever tried coconut milk in her latte. But nothing from Cristiano.

Her stomach sank. Disappointment settled deeply in her chest. But it was quickly replaced by a new sensation: relief. She'd taken the first step, broken the wall of silence between them, and Cristiano had chosen not to communicate in return. At least now she knew where she stood. She didn't need to wonder anymore. As difficult as it was to know things were truly over, she was glad at least for some certainty.

She looked back at Maxine's messages, no longer distracted by thoughts of Cristiano and able to pay them the attention they deserved.

Are you okay, hon? So sorry about Rob! What a jerk. I know you well enough to know you're probably embarrassed about it, but you're literally my hero right now.

She smiled to herself, her mortification of having made a spectacle of herself dissipating slightly. She typed a response.

Sorry for being silent. I must've fallen asleep as soon as I got home. Of course I'm embarrassed, but at least you're proud of me.

She sent the message and went to put her phone away, then on second thought sent a text to her mom, Mallory. *Yes. And it's yummy.*

She heard the sound of a key in the door then and jumped with surprise. As she turned to look over her shoulder, she saw Bryn enter the apartment, dressed in workout gear, her cheeks pink, hairline sweaty, and face grinning widely. Keira realized then that she was not alone. Felix was in tow. For an older gentleman he certainly looked all right in workout gear. He reminded her a little of the before model from an ad for male hair dye.

"You're up," Bryn said to Keira with a smile. "How was the party?"

"Could've been better," Keira murmured in reply. "Where have you two been?"

Bryn went over to the sink to fill up her empty water bottle. It was Felix who answered Keira's question.

"We just went for a jog," he said.

Keira had to stop herself from exclaiming, "At your age?" Instead, she managed to censor herself and instead asked, "At this time of the morning?"

"Best time for it," Felix replied. He raised one of his legs, resting it on a kitchen stool and stretching to touch his toes.

He was fitter than Keira, that much was evident. She'd let everything deteriorate in that department and her waistline was starting to suffer for it. It was all well and good eating and drinking to her heart's content when she was hiking up Italian mountainsides, but now that her evenings consisted of binge-watching TV and eating pretzels, it wasn't so great. She poked her stomach. It was definitely squishier than it used to be. She'd have to do something about that soon.

Bryn turned back from the sink and took a long swig from her bottle. "Have you heard from Mom?"

"Just some random text about coconut milk latte," Keira replied.

Bryn laughed. "She's losing her mind. She was supposed to let you know about dinner tonight."

"Oh," Keira replied.

"Well?" Bryn probed. "What do you say? Swanson ladies dinner date?"

"Isn't Felix invited?" Keira asked, curiously. Mallory seemed to love Felix; either that or she was just very relieved that Bryn had finally started a stable relationship.

Felix switched to stretching his other leg. He glanced at Keira, his hands outstretched clasping the toe of his sneaker. "I've got plans with my own family tonight. It's my parents' wedding anniversary."

Once again, Keira had to bite her tongue to stop from blurting out something rude. But she really was surprised that Felix's parents were alive and kicking. They must be well into their eighties, the age Keira's grandparents would have been had either still been alive.

"That's lovely," she managed to say.

"What shall I tell Mom?" Bryn asked.

"Tell her okay," Keira replied.

Maybe some mollycoddling could help kick-start her out of her funk. There really was nothing like Mallory's maternal cloying to remind Keira how important her independence was.

Bryn and Felix exchanged a nod and then headed for the door.

"Where are you going?" Keira asked.

"Second five K," Bryn replied.

"Ten before breakfast has always been my motto," Felix added.

They waved and swirled out the door. Keira blinked at it. It was hard to believe that *anyone* could be that physically active, let alone a sixty-something man. She wondered how long it took someone to train to run 10k and realized it wouldn't take that long at all. Certainly less than a year. Felix could have started his fitness regime on his sixtieth birthday for all she knew. It was never too late to make a change.

She realized, suddenly, that she needed to stop sitting around feeling sorry for herself. Overcome by a surge of motivation, Keira grasped her work bag and pulled out her notebook. She quickly wrote a list of all the things she needed to change in her life, including losing a couple of extra pounds and getting her roots touched up. She scanned the list and realized there was one very important change she needed to make to get her life back on track, and that was getting herself into her own apartment. The longer she stayed sleeping on Bryn's couch, the harder it was becoming to ever imagine herself being independent, standing on her own two feet again.

She fetched her laptop and went onto a real estate website. She hadn't checked apartment prices for at least a couple of years, having been settled with Zach for so long, and the prices made her eyes water. But if she added up her work bonuses and the several grand she'd saved just from not having to pay rent or for any of her food for the last few months, she might just be able to scrape together enough to put down a deposit. On paper she looked like a safe bet, since she had a steady job with a decent income. She started to feel the first glimmer of hope in days.

She scrolled through all the apartments, looking for one to rent within her price range. Most of them looked a little worse for wear, but she liked DIY and didn't mind having a fixer-upper. She just wanted something that was her own, somewhere she could call home after spending weeks on end in hotel rooms.

At last, an apartment caught her eye. A one-bed, one-bath condo farther west from Manhattan than she usually went. From the photos it looked like it had been a sad divorcé's downsizer, but Keira could see past the drab, unloved decor. The windows were huge, the ceilings high. Without the graying carpet it would look even more spacious. The building had laundry facilities in the basement, and it was less than a mile from a subway station.

It felt like fate.

Keira grabbed her phone and punched in the agent's number. After a few rings, a croaky voice answered, an older woman with a decades-developed smoker's rasp.

"I'm inquiring about the apartment on your website," she said, explaining which specific one she was interested in.

"Oh yeah, that one's a beaut," the woman replied. "Great location. How tall are you?"

Keira was taken aback by the question. "Why?"

"'Cause the last two guys I showed it to were the size of basketball players and wanted more space. Waste of everyone's time. And time is money, kiddo. So? How tall?"

"Five two," Keira said.

"Perfect," the woman rasped. "When d'ya wanna look?"

Keira thought of her job, of the long hours she often had to work at *Viatorum*. "A weekend would be better."

"Whatcha doin' today?" came the woman's response. "I had a cancellation so could fit you in."

"Today?" Keira repeated, surprised. It wasn't like she had anything else to do. "Okay, yes. Today is fine!"

They made the necessary arrangements and Keira hung up the call, feeling a little dazed from the speed with which it had all happened. It really did feel like fate.

*

Keira left the subway, finding herself in an unfamiliar but rather pleasant part of New York. It was one of the things about the city she loved so much, how it changed, evolved, and developed so constantly it was always reinventing itself. Not that long ago this area must have been a bit rundown and the public hadn't yet caught on, because there was no way she'd be able to afford to rent a place here otherwise!

She hurried along the sidewalk, scanning the door numbers as she went, searching for the correct building. As she drew closer to the correct number, she noticed a woman standing ahead in a fuchsia pink two-piece and matching heels, smoking a cigarette. That must be the real estate agent she spoke to on the phone.

The woman turned, presumably at the sound of Keira's footsteps, and threw her cigarette to the ground. She put it out with the toe of her shoe and headed toward the door, gesturing for Keira to follow her, blowing smoke from the side of her lips as she went.

"Let's get inside," she called out when Keira was still a few paces away. "I'm freezing my butt off out here."

Keira blinked in surprise at how rapidly things continued to move. Without even introductions, she followed the woman inside the apartment building.

Inside, it was as dingy as Keira had expected, but the staircase was in one piece and the elevator smelled fine. They went up to the thirteenth floor and Keira was pleased to see there was no graffiti anywhere in the corridor they emerged into.

The real estate agent put a key in the lock of a plain white door and then pushed it open.

The smell of dust wafted out. It smelled like the condo hadn't been vacuumed for years. They stepped inside.

"The landlord lived here for a bit before moving to another place and renting this out. He's a bachelor," the agent said, wiping her fingers across the balustrade and picking up dust. "You can probably tell."

But Keira didn't care about the layer of dust. She didn't even care about how much smaller the apartment was in real life compared to the pictures, or how the wallpaper was covered in smudgy handprints. She could see past all of that. The condo to her meant freedom, independence, the beginning of her life. A reboot. An anchor.

"I love it!" she cried, clapping her hands.

The agent didn't seem moved by her gushing. "Good," she said simply. "Bedroom's through there. That's the reason it's cheap. Not

17

enough room for a proper double, just one of those European-sized ones. But you're short so you'll fit fine."

Keira peered into the bedroom. It was indeed little more than a closet. But what else did she need from a bedroom than a place to sleep? It wasn't like she had a partner to share her bed with, it would just be her. Her and maybe a cat...

"Looks big enough for me," she said. "I don't actually own a bed so it will just be a case of getting something that fits."

The real estate agent nodded in her characteristic lackluster way. "Great. Wanna rent it?"

Keira needed a moment to think. This was happening too fast. She ducked back out of the bedroom into the living area and walked over to the large windows, looking out at the view. She could see Central Park from here.

Suddenly she could imagine herself sitting by this window, gazing out at the streets, drinking coffee, writing. It was like her own Paris hotel window. Perfect for her. She didn't need anything fancy, not when she was abroad for work so often. She just needed somewhere to call her own. A fresh start.

She swirled to face the fuchsia-clad real estate agent. "Yes. I'll take it."

CHAPTER THREE

Mallory leaned across the table and filled Keira's now empty glass with more rosé. Keira grimaced. She didn't care for the sickly sweet pink wine her mother favored, but there wasn't much she could do about it. When it came to Mallory Swanson, refusal was futile.

Bryn caught Keira's eye from across the table and smirked. She hated the pink wine just as much as Keira did. At least it provided them with a private joke they could share.

"So Keira," Mallory said, addressing her youngest daughter.

Keira broke her gaze from Bryn to regard Mallory. She could tell by the way her mother's eyes were slightly narrowed, and the way her wine glass was askew in her hands, that she was slightly tipsy. Which meant that she was about to ask something very personal, as was her way when she'd had a glass or two.

Keira braced herself. "Yes, Mother?"

"Have you heard from Cristiano?"

There it was. The gut punch.

Before Keira had a chance to even groan, Mallory flinched and flashed angry eyes at Bryn.

"Don't kick me, young lady!" she exclaimed. "If I don't ask she doesn't tell. How else am I supposed to know what's going on in my daughter's life? One minute he was Mr. Right and then he was Mr. Gone. I want to know what happened."

Petulance was another one of Mallory's tipsy habits.

Keira sighed. "It's okay. It's about time I talked about what happened." She put her wine glass down. At least if she was the one commanding the conversation she'd have an excuse not to drink any more rosé. "I haven't heard from him since I broke it off. I really thought we'd be friends. It felt like a mature separation, you know? Like we could both tell it wasn't right. But then he disappeared off the face of the earth. No communication whatsoever. I mean, am I an idiot for ever thinking you can be friends with an ex? The same thing happened with Shane."

"Oh, darling, I'm not the one to ask," Mallory replied. "You know too well how disastrous my love life has been."

If Keira had a bingo card for things her mom discussed when she was drinking, she'd probably have ticked all the boxes by now. Career. Tick. Painful broken heart. Tick. And now, the real kicker: Dad.

Keira knew the story all too well, but that didn't stop Mallory from bringing it up constantly. He was her one true love, they were young but thought it would work, he couldn't handle the responsibility of children, he'd left her destitute in a big city with two young kids. Though she'd never met her dad, Keira was absolutely certain his absence played a role in her own inability to sustain a happy relationship. And he was *definitely* the reason Bryn was setting up house with an old man.

Mallory waved her glass in front of her face, sloshing some pink liquid onto the table in front of her. "I will say this though. Broken hearts, like broken bones, are stronger once they're repaired."

Keira quirked an eyebrow. That was actually quite insightful coming from Mallory.

"Who are you quoting that from, Mom?" Bryn piped up. "Oprah Winfrey?"

"I don't remember who," Mallory snapped. "It might have been in a fortune cookie. It doesn't matter. The point is, you will get over this and you will learn something and you will heal and your heart will go on."

"Ooh, I know that one. That one's Celine Dion," Bryn said.

Mallory frowned at her. "Will you stop with your jokes, Bryn! I'm trying to make Keira feel better."

"You are, Mom," Keira said meaningfully, speaking for the first time in ages. "You're actually helping a ton. Bryn is too, in her own way." She smiled at her sister. Bryn had put up with a lot from Keira over the last few weeks, from her moping around all day in unwashed clothes to her short temper. Now felt like a good time to let them know about what had happened with the real estate agent earlier that day. "Actually, I have a bit of news. Good news."

"Oh?" they both asked in unison.

Keira felt suddenly shy. Renting a condo was such a big step for her, for all of them really. It would mark her transition, finally, from young adult to woman. For Mallory, it would be the end of her constant worry about her youngest getting along in the world. For Bryn, it would mean the return of her own independence, the lessening of responsibility, the lightening of the burden she'd always had to carry as the older of the two sisters.

"I've put a deposit down to rent my own apartment."

There was a moment of stunned silence. Then Bryn began to whoop. Mallory broke into a wide grin.

"Darling, have you really?" she asked.

Keira smiled shyly and nodded. "Yup."

Bryn was out of her seat suddenly. She came up around Keira and threw her arms about. "Oh THANK GOD!" she cried.

Keira laughed in her tight embrace. "Okay, okay, I know I've been a pain, but really!"

Bryn released her grip a little. "It's not that you've been a pain," she said. "It's just that Felix... well, he asked me to get a place with him. I've been dragging my feet..."

"I knew it!" Keira exclaimed.

From the other side of the table, Mallory began to cry. "My two girls, growing up so fast."

Of course, the last box on the bingo board could now be ticked. Cry!

*

Keira headed out into the cold evening, pulling her coat about her. The dinner with her mom and Bryn had been rejuvenating. She'd enjoyed it far more than she'd expected.

Bryn had headed off to Felix's for the night, so Keira would have the apartment to herself. She was tired, though, and felt like going straight to bed. She'd be back in the office tomorrow and wanted to be fresh for it. She'd been a grump for the last few weeks. Hopefully her positive attitude would carry over until tomorrow.

The subway sign appeared up ahead. As she headed toward it, Keira felt a vibration in her pocket. Her cell phone. She reached inside and took it out.

To her surprise, this time it was a text from Cristiano. Her heart seemed to stop beating as she opened it up.

Whoever this is, leave Cristiano alone. He's moved on.

Keira stared at the message, blinking in shock. It wasn't from Cristiano at all, but from someone using his phone. A new girlfriend?

Her stomach sank. All the good work that had been done that evening seemed to suddenly unravel and spool inside of her. How could he have moved on so quickly? After all those conversations they'd had about him only wanting to date women he could imagine marrying. How many were there for him to have found a new one in such a short space of time! Being marriage material in Cristiano's eyes clearly didn't mean that much after all. Had Keira been duped?

She thrust her phone back into her purse. Fuming, she hurried down the subway steps and on to the waiting train. She slumped into a seat and gazed at the blackness out the window.

Her mind raced a mile a minute, picking apart all the times they'd spent together, searching for new meaning, new clues in the moments they were together.

But the more she thought, the more her anger lessened. Instead of holding on to the worst possible scenario her mind could conjure—that Cristiano had lied to her about being careful with his heart—she managed to talk herself down to a place of reason. Sometimes the rebound relationship was the best relationship. He'd been her rebound from Shane and the time they'd spent together had been wonderful. Perhaps this new woman was just his rebound rather than his next wife. Perhaps he'd learned that from Keira, that sometimes it was okay to be with a person just because you wanted to, rather than always having some grand plan in place.

She remembered Mallory's words, about each relationship being an opportunity to learn and grow, to move onward and upward. Cristiano might indeed be going through the same thing. And Keira could feel, tangibly, that she was as well. Rather than holding on to her fury, to her bruised ego, it had only taken her the subway ride to start to let it go.

She got off the train and headed back up to street level, exiting the subway a wiser woman than she'd been when she entered. When she'd gotten on the train she was upset but as she left, she was relieved. This was the real line in the sand with her Cristiano. This was the real ending. It was time to move on, once and for all.

CHAPTER FOUR

Keira wrapped her knuckles against Elliot's office door. It was open, but she still felt the need to be polite.

"Morning, Keira," he said, turning over his shoulder to look at her. "Come in, come in."

Keira entered, taking a seat opposite him. She always felt intimidated by Elliot's office, like she was a school kid facing the principal.

"Everything okay?" he asked, tipping his gaze up to meet hers.

Keira swallowed the little lump of nerves that always formed in her throat when speaking to her boss. "Yes. I wanted to apologize, actually."

"For what?" Elliot replied, frowning.

"For the last few weeks since I got back from France. I haven't been my best." Now that she'd begun speaking, she wanted to get it all out, and her words spilled off her tongue quickly. "And I know I've been avoiding picking a location for the new assignment, I think I just needed time after Cristiano. I was worried, you know? Another assignment, another broken heart. But I should have just been honest rather than avoiding the topic, so I'm sorry." She took a deep breath, then smiled, feeling satisfied to have finally aired her worries.

"Oh," Elliot replied, a bit blankly. "To be honest, I hadn't noticed."

Keira frowned. "You hadn't? But you've emailed me pretty much every day asking where I wanted to go on my next assignment."

Elliot shrugged. "I send a lot of emails, Keira. Look, I'm writing one to you as we speak. Guess I don't need to now." He clicked some buttons and then folded his arms and looked at her.

There was a long pause. Keira blinked. "Well, what was in the email?"

"Oh yes," Elliot said, snapping back to attention. "It was about your new assignment abroad."

"My…" Keira let that sink in. She narrowed her eyes. "You mean you've decided where it is?"

They were supposed to consult her! That was the agreement they'd come to, that she'd pick her own locations from now on. Elliot had agreed to it. How could they go back on that now?

"Well, I asked for your input," Elliot replied simply. "And I didn't get it so I asked Heather to go ahead and book something anyway. This is a fast-paced environment, Keira. If people don't get back to me, I'm not going to sit around waiting forever."

He sounded completely emotionless. But Keira felt totally betrayed. Not only did they exploit her heart for entertainment, but now they were going back on their word? Frustration boiled inside of her.

"Where are you sending me?" she asked in a clipped voice.

Elliot looked at his watch. "I'll tell you in the team meeting." Then he clapped his hands. "Come on."

Keira's head spun from her talk with Elliot. It hadn't gone how she'd expected at all. She watched Elliot waltz from the room, her mind reeling. Had he forgotten their arrangement or did he just not care? And what about Nina? She, at the very least, should have known not to plow ahead without Keira's consent! She was supposed to be Keira's friend, be on her side, but as she progressed through the *Viatorum* ranks she'd started siding more and more with Elliot.

Dazed, Keira stood and followed Elliot from the room, into the adjoining conference room. Other writers had started to file in, coffees in hand, and take seats. Keira realized that there were yet more new faces among them. She'd been so cloistered in her own office for the last few weeks she hadn't even noticed or bothered to speak to any of them. She felt guilty about that now. It wasn't that long ago that she was a brand new writer here, desperate for assurance and friendship. She resolved to try harder.

"How's everyone doing today?" she asked a group of newbies, directing her question at a young woman with long braided hair and a septum ring.

The girl blinked, as though shocked Keira was speaking to her. "Good," she said in a high-pitched squeak. "It's assignment day, so I'm looking forward to finding out my new assignment."

The rest of the group just nodded. One of them even blushed. Keira had never had such an effect on people before. It was easy to forget that she was in a senior role here, that she was a writer who breezed in to meetings and then was out of the office for weeks at a time. They probably thought of her what she thought of Elliot, or of Lance once upon a time. It was the most peculiar feeling.

"I'm Keira, by the way," she said, reaching out to shake the girl's hand.

"Yes, I know," the girl said. "I'm Meredith." She had a warm smile.

Keira took a seat beside her. "You're new, right?"

"Ish," Meredith replied. "I started while you were in France." She looked suddenly shy. "I loved your article, by the way."

"Oh," Keira said, "thanks. I'm kinda trying to move on from all that."

"All what? You mean Romance Guru articles?" Meredith's eyes widened. "You can't! They're amazing!"

Keira didn't have time to reply because Elliot began the meeting.

She felt a pit of dread open up in her stomach. Whatever they had planned for her, she had to be strong. If she didn't want to do it, she'd quit. It was that simple. Though of course, easier said than done.

"Let's start with a huge round of applause for Meredith," Elliot started. "Her New York City graffiti tour e-article was a smash hit."

Everyone clapped and Meredith beamed. Keira felt happy for her. When she'd started at the magazine, it had been under Joshua's command. He made everyone feel like a failure. The work environment was much better now, much more supportive.

Elliot continued. "Next, I think you're all interested to know where our Romance Guru is off to for our special December publication."

"Lapland?" one of the new kids said.

"See if she can seduce Santa," a fresh-faced boy added.

Everyone laughed. Everyone but Keira.

"No," Elliot said. "We decided on something a little different."

This was it. Crunch time. Every muscle in Keira's body tensed.

"We're sending her on a cruise of Scandinavia. This time, the assignment is to prove that someone suffering from a breakup can avoid a knee-jerk rebound affair. This time, we want our Guru to *not* fall in love."

Keira was stunned. She'd had the words *I quit* waiting on the tip of her tongue, but now she had to swallow them down.

"Impossible," the fresh-faced joker from before said. "She'll fall for the tour guide, and you all know it."

He was teasing, of course, but Keira was in too much shock to pay him any attention at all.

"Which is why we're not having a tour guide," Elliot added. He looked at Keira. "You have fifteen days. Other than the course of the ship—which will take you through Denmark, Finland, and Sweden—the rest is up to you. You'll be navigating yourself entirely."

Keira was lost for words. As it began to sink in, she felt her worries melt away. She wasn't going to be expected to bruise her heart this time! Sure, she would still have to dig deep and make her article personal, but she wouldn't need to put herself on the line.

The joker had one last quip to make. "So, basically she's just writing a travel article?"

Everyone laughed. But Keira only had one thing to say, only one word to describe what her mind was imagining; the Northern Lights, fjords, snow-capped mountains, and meatballs galore! Finally, she managed to untie her tongue. "Wow."

CHAPTER FIVE

Keira was filled with excitement as she hurried into Bryn's apartment after work that evening. Her sister wasn't yet home, so there was no one to tell her news to. Instead, she rummaged beneath Bryn's bed for her trusty suitcase, surprised that she was so pleased to be packing it once again. She'd been utterly convinced she never wanted to do this again, and yet here she was, thrilled to be traveling abroad for work once more.

Her phone pinged a message then, and she looked to see it was from her mom.

What's the difference between a cortado and a flat-white?

Keira laughed and called Mallory's number. As soon as Mallory answered, she began talking about coffee, clearly assuming that to be the purpose of her daughter's call.

"I mean is it *just* the cup size? It has to be more than that, doesn't it?" she mused aloud.

"Mom, I'm going abroad again," Keira said, paying no attention to the coffee conversation.

"You are?" Mallory said, sounding surprised. "But I thought you were putting your foot down about the Romance Guru articles."

"I was," Keira said, sitting on the edge of Bryn's bed with a light sigh. "But this one is different."

"In what way?"

"The whole point is to not rebound this time. I mean, it's exactly what I need, don't you think? A chance to work on myself. To be alone. I've jumped from one guy to the next for too long now."

"When do you leave?"

"Tomorrow. Typical *Viatorum* can't give me more than a day's notice of anything."

There was a slight pause. "Well, I'm happy for you, darling," Mallory finally said.

Keira distinctly caught the edge in her voice. "What is it?"

"Nothing," Mallory protested. "I just said I was happy for you."

"There's a but coming…" Keira said.

"No, there isn't."

27

"Yes, there is. Mom, I've been your daughter for twenty-eight years. I know when there's a but coming."

Mallory sighed. "Fine. I was going to say, 'But what about Christmas?'"

"Ohh," Keira said, relieved. She'd thought Mallory was going to make some comment about how Keira would fail her assignment, how she was always destined to fall for the wrong man, never marry, never make her a grandma, all that stuff. With a chuckle, Keira assured her, "I'll be back for Christmas."

"So it's only a short trip this time?"

"Just over two weeks. You have nothing to worry about. I'll be there dutifully on Christmas Eve like always."

"Good," Mallory replied. "So back to my question. What *is* the difference between a cortado and a flat-white?"

Keira laughed. "Bye, Mom. I love you."

She ended the call and went about packing her case. She piled inside of it all her warmest clothing, sweaters and scarves, extra-thick socks and thermal-lined leggings. Then she added her makeup bag, toiletries, some waterproof boots, and a fresh supply of notebooks and pens.

The door opened then, and she heard Bryn call out, "I'm home!"

Keira jumped up and ran to meet her sister.

"Guess what?" she exclaimed, as Bryn flung her keys into the bowl by the door and kicked off her shoes.

Her sister looked up. "What?"

"I'm going to *Scandinavia*! On a cruise ship!"

Bryn's eyes widened. "Really? Wow! That's awesome."

"And I don't have to fall in love with anyone either."

"Oh good. That's exactly what you need."

She seemed genuinely thrilled for Keira, and again Keira saw a more mature side to her sister, as if the edges of her competitiveness had begun to soften.

"But what about your apartment?" Bryn asked. "Won't there be a lease to sign before you leave?"

"Good point," Keira said, feeling reality bring her back down from her fantasy land. "I'll have to call the real estate agent now and arrange it."

She went into the bedroom and fetched her cell phone, then called the number. The real estate agent answered in her raspy smoker's voice and Keira instantly recalled her fuchsia-pink suit.

"Kid, I was about to call you," she said. "I need you to make an appointment to come in and sign the lease."

Keira laughed. "That's exactly what I was calling for. I've got to go abroad for work, for fifteen days. So I'll have to get the paperwork signed before I go, or it will have to wait until I get back."

The agent sighed loudly. "Kid, you're killing me. You're telling me I've got to drop everything so I can get it sorted out for you? I usually need a week to get the paperwork arranged."

Keira felt her heart sink. She felt terrible for being an imposition, but at the same time the real estate agent was being pretty rude, making it seem like her simple request was completely unacceptable. "Maybe it would be easier to wait until I'm back, in that case?" she suggested. Then she added, slightly sarcastically, "I'd hate to put you out."

"I can speak to the landlord," the woman replied with a huge sigh. "See what he thinks. But I know he wanted to move fast with this and if you're dragging your heels…"

Keira grew even more frustrated. "I can come in now and sign the paperwork. But you said it would take a week to prepare. But fifteen days is too slow? Seems like you have a pretty inflexible schedule."

As soon as she finished speaking, Keira felt shocked with herself. It wasn't often that she was so outspoken. But if it all fell through, what were the chances of her finding another apartment like that one? The only reason she'd been able to afford the rent in the first place was because of the small bedroom. But there must be other short people out there who'd snap it up while she was away! To lose it now would be too cruel a twist of fate.

"Fine," the agent said. "I'll bust my balls to get everything ready in time for your trip abroad." Her voice dripped with disdain.

Through gritted teeth, Keira muttered, "Thank you."

She ended the call, stressed by the conversation. Then she became acutely aware of voices coming from the living area of Bryn's apartment. Someone was there. She peered out the bedroom door.

Keira's mouth dropped open. There, standing in Bryn's kitchen, was Zach. His nose was still bandaged from when Cristiano had broken it, and faded bruises were still visible beneath his eyes.

Bryn, with folded arms, was glaring at him with her fiercest overprotective-sister expression.

"She's not going to want to see you," Keira heard her say.

The bedroom door creaked then, and Zach and Bryn looked over at her. Sheepishly, Keira came into the living room.

"Zach," she said, meekly. "What are you doing here?"

He smiled at the sight of her, though his features were mostly obscured by the bandages. "What, no hug?"

Keira stood still. There would definitely be no hug for her ex-boyfriend, especially after the tricks he'd played in France and how rude he'd been with withholding her money. Bryn rolled her eyes in disdain.

Zachary let his arms drop. "Right," he said stiffly. "Look, I won't take up too much of your time. I just wanted to give you this."

Keira watched him produce something from his pocket. A slip of paper, the same size and shape as a check. She wouldn't let herself believe that it was one, though. He handed it to her.

"What is it?" she said, still not believing.

"Your half of the deposit," he explained. Then he sighed, sounding a little strained. "Look, I spoke to my cousin, told him it wasn't fair to take that money off you. So he agreed to give your portion back."

"Really?" Keira said, her eyebrows rising. Finally, she took the paper and turned it in her hands so that it was the right way up. It was, indeed, the full portion of her contribution to the deposit. She looked up again at Zach. "Wow. Thank you. I really appreciate this."

Bryn scoffed. She clearly thought Keira was being too soft on Zach. Keira herself admitted she probably was. But it was just her way. She wasn't one to hold grudges. Once a wrong had been righted, there didn't seem much point in doing so. Just a whole lot of wasted energy. Like Bryn and Maxine; no one had any clue how that animosity had started but neither was ever going to let it go.

"I also wanted to say sorry," Zach continued. "I know what happened in France was crazy. I spoke to my mom and Ruth and my cousin and Shelby and David and my therapist, and there's unanimous agreement that I was acting like a lunatic." He smiled shyly. "I'm really sorry if I creeped you out."

"Okay," Keira replied. "I appreciate you saying that. And the nose. I'm really sorry about that."

"God, I deserved it!" Zach laughed. "If some guy had done that while you were my girlfriend I'd have reacted the same way. I just hope it heals well. Gives me character."

"I'm sure it will," Keira admitted, smiling shyly.

Bryn let another noise of disgust come from the back of her throat. Her arms crossed even tighter against her chest.

"Are we done now?" she asked, coldly. "We have things to be getting on with."

Zach flicked his gaze from Keira to Bryn. "Almost," he told her. "Can we have a bit of privacy though? Then I'll get out of your hair."

Bryn looked at Keira. One of her eyebrows was raised. Her lips were pursed. Everything in her stance screamed *don't fall for his tricks*. But she finally relented, heading into her bedroom and closing the door.

Keira looked at Zach. "So?"

"So..." Zach began. He drummed his fingers on the kitchen counter. Whatever he had to say clearly wasn't coming easy. "Keira, I know I've been a jerk."

Keira held her tongue, though she really wanted to scream out, "Finally you admit it!"

"And... the thing is... I've been acting that way because I care for you so deeply." He gazed up at her, his eyes like big pools of sorrow. "When I gave you that ultimatum I really, really didn't think you'd choose your job."

Keira recalled, painfully, the complete misunderstanding that had resulted in her and Zach's relationship ending. She'd never thought he'd follow through with his threat to end it with her, but sleeping with his sister's maid of honor had really been the nail in the coffin of their relationship.

"I didn't think you'd sleep with the first woman who'd agree to it," Keira replied tersely.

"I know, I know," Zach said, looking away and letting out a painful sigh. "I was hurting. That's all I can say. I was so sad that you put something else before me that I wanted to put myself before you, put my needs first. It was... well, it was a shitty way to treat you."

Keira just mumbled in agreement. In a few days' time, once the dust had settled, she'd be grateful for Zach apologizing, but right now it was just stirring up a ton of feelings Keira didn't have time to process.

"Okay, well thanks, I guess," she finally said. "But, like Bryn said, we've got stuff to do."

"Sure," Zach said, looking over at the bedroom door that was now standing ajar. Bryn was evidently spying on them. He cast his gaze back at Keira and suddenly blurted, "Can you give me another chance?"

Keira's eyebrows shot up her forehead. "What?"

"Please," Zach said. "I don't want to beg but I will. I know I don't deserve you, especially after how I've behaved. But you drive me crazy because I love you. I can see that now."

Keira was stunned. In the two years she and Zach had been together, love had never come into the equation. They'd been friends, partners, and equals, sure, but *actually* in love? She couldn't be certain. They'd never said it, had never felt the need to speak those words. To hear him say them now touched her.

"Zach..." Keira began. "That's sweet of you to say. But... I can't. I'm sorry."

She watched his chest deflate like a balloon, the hope sucked out of him with her words.

"I really blew it, huh?" he said, sounding depressed.

She shook her head. "It's not that. I've been through a lot over the last few months. I've grown and learned and changed. I know what I want now."

"And it's not me," he finished for her.

Keira nodded sadly. "I'm sorry. But no, it's not you."

"So no amount of begging for forgiveness will work?" Zach asked.

"No," Keira told him, soft but firm. "It's not about that. I'm not waiting to forgive you. I just don't... I don't want you like that. But we can be friends."

"Sure," Zach said, gazing at his feet. "We can be friends."

Keira led a dejected Zachary from Bryn's house. Self-pity certainly wasn't going to help his case. She hoped he'd bounce back soon enough, and learn that he hadn't really blown it with her, they just weren't right, and that there'd be some other woman out there who was right for him.

As soon as she closed the door, Bryn hurried out of the bedroom.

"Sis!" she exclaimed, raising a hand for a high five. "That was awesome!"

Keira felt the edges of her lips twitch up. She clapped Bryn's hand. "It was?"

"Yes! You totally held your own." Bryn slung an arm around Keira's shoulder. "You're going to be just fine on this assignment, I know you are."

Keira smiled, feeling filled with strength and resolve. Bryn was right. She was going to smash this assignment.

CHAPTER SIX

Bright and early the next morning, Keira received a grumpy call from the real estate agent saying the paperwork was ready for her to sign. Relieved, Keira hurried to her office and scribbled her name on the lease, before racing off for the airport.

Her head was spinning so much from having to rapidly sort things out, that it was only as she plopped herself into her seat on the airplane that it really sank in where she was and what was going on. At least this felt familiar to her now, being on a plane. It was nowhere near as intimidating as it once had been. For the first time, Keira felt much more positive about the future.

She couldn't help but recall how the last time she'd boarded a plane Cristiano had been in the seat beside her. She could still remember the thrilling excitement she'd felt as they neared New York City, and the way his eyes had widened at the sight of a million lights below. That was all gone now. All she had left now were the memories. And for the first time since she'd ended things with Cristiano, her memories of him no longer stung. The thorny layer that had been around them before, causing her pain any time she tried to touch them, had finally gone.

She thought of the text from Cristiano's new girlfriend, the one she'd been agonizing over. It felt so stupid to her now to have been that worked up over him seeing someone else. Of course it didn't mean their relationship had meant nothing to him, it just meant that he was moving on with someone new.

The plane took to the skies, and the sensation of soaring made her stomach flip. Being so high above the world made her feel so free, so bold and independent. She smiled to herself and looked in her carry-on bag for the details of the upcoming cruise.

Heather had outdone herself this time. The itinerary was *laminated*. Probably as an attempt to mitigate against Keira's tendency to spill coffee and fall off gondolas into canals. Heather had also bound the pages. It reminded Keira of something she would have produced in college, and she smirked to herself.

Keira flicked straight past the pages of important contact numbers—noting with a wry smile the empty space where a tour guide's name and number would normally be—and skipped straight to the juicy details of the cruise. She'd hardly had time to get her head around the fact she was going on a cruise, that she'd be on a huge boat in the open sea. It would be a brand new experience for her. Her stomach leapt with anticipation. She glanced through the list of locations: Copenhagen, Denmark. Helsinki, Finland. Stockholm, Sweden.

Heather wasn't one for adornment and there were no pictures included to further whet Keira's appetite—*too expensive to print in color*, she thought in Heather's voice—so she took her tablet from her bag and began to search online.

The images were stunning. Unlike the European cities she'd visited thus far, the buildings in the Scandinavian countries were different, peaked like alpine lodges. And there were vast swaths of countryside, beautiful evergreen trees, lakes of deep blue, and craggy mountains. She could hardly sit through the rest of the plane ride; she wanted to be there now!

Napping was always a good way to pass the time, so Keira settled into her airplane seat and let herself drift off to sleep.

She dreamed she was standing on the edge of a cliff, looking out at the ocean, deep blue and calm. Through the waves she saw a school of dolphins, jumping up before disappearing again. She watched, amazed, as they leaped in strange formations. It was almost like they were dancing, or performing synchronized routines for her. As though trying to impress her.

Keira noticed something peculiar about the dolphins then, about their faces. Even from this distance, she could make out their strangely human expressions, and the varying shades of their eyes. One had the same piercing blue eyes of Shane, and his crooked, cheeky smile to match. Another had deep chocolate eyes, a softness in its expression that reminded her of Cristiano. Yet another had a lost expression, with a look of mourning and regret behind its eyes. Zachary.

No sooner had she made these connections than their graceful acrobatics transformed into something new. Not a coordinated routine anymore, but something aggressive. A display of masculinity. The Cristiano dolphin plowed headfirst into the Zachary one, busting his nose, or snout, or whatever it was called on a dolphin. The Zachary one hit back, swishing his tail at both Cristiano and Shane. Shane just stood on the back of his tail, flapping his great flippers like this was all a huge joke. Then they piled in on one another, ripping shreds from one another as she watched on horrified, the blue ocean turning red before her eyes.

She tried to call out, "Stop! It's not a competition!" But her voice was drowned out by the winds.

Then a new danger took her focus. Racing through the waves toward the sparring dolphins was an enormous whale. She didn't know who this whale was, a stranger, but he moved with purpose and killer determination. Her dolphin-exes were so busy attacking one another they didn't even notice the whale approach until it was on top of them. In one huge mouthful, the whale ate all three dolphins up. Then it disappeared beneath the waves, making a whirlpool as it went, leaving nothing behind but bloody water to show anything had ever happened there.

Keira startled awake. She was sweating, and her neck was stuck in a painful position. She rubbed it, adjusting to the brightness of the cabin, to the smells and sounds of the airplane in flight around her; rustling chip packets, the merry chatter of excited vacationers, the whirr of powerful engines. Finally coming back to herself, Keira began to chuckle.

What a strange mind she had! To turn her exes into dolphins like that. But she wondered who the whale signified. Not a new boyfriend, she assured herself. That wasn't the plan, not at all. She decided the whale signified her career, the way she was going to put it first and forget all traces of her ex-boyfriends in order to excel. There was no rebound affair on the horizon. At least, that was the plan...

CHAPTER SEVEN

Keira landed in Berlin, Germany—where the ship would be embarking from—several hours later. Her mind hadn't quite gotten over the hilariously strange dream it had shown her on the airplane, and it took a bit of concentration to switch focus to the real world.

She maneuvered through Berlin Tegel Airport, collecting her case and following the signs that she hoped were taking her to the exit. It felt good to be on her own this time. No guide to show her around, or take any of the responsibility off her shoulders. This time it was just her, and it made her feel powerful.

She made it out of the airport and hailed a cab. The driver was in his fifties or so, with graying hair and a stern expression. But his attitude was far friendlier than his fierce expression would have indicated.

"You're going on the Scandinavian cruise?" he asked in perfect English and just the smallest hint of an accent.

"I am." Keira beamed. "I'm so excited."

"I'd love to go one day," he said. "It's a bit too expensive for a taxi driver though. Do you mind me asking your profession?"

"Oh, I'm a writer," Keira told him. "This is all paid for by the company."

"You're very lucky," he said. "What do you write?"

"Travel articles. Well, sort of. They're a bit of a mixture. Travel and romance."

From the back seat, Keira saw his reflection in the rearview mirror as he raised his eyebrows.

"Travel and romance?"

"I know, it sounds strange. But it's more like personal accounts of the countries and my experiences within them, with dating and trying new things, meeting new men. It's a bit of a mishmash but I'm starting to get a loyal following."

"Weird question," he said. "You don't write for that Latin-sounding magazine, do you? Viaduct, or whatever?"

"*Viatorum*," she told him, a little surprised he'd have heard of her New York City publication all the way over in Germany. But then again, they also e-published and anyone in the world could access the content online. "Have you heard of it?"

"My wife loves it," he said, with an air of frustration. "You're the one on the cover, aren't you? I recognize your face now."

The cover. With Cristiano. Keira groaned. She'd known at the time the image would come to haunt her one day, but she'd let Nina and Elliot have their way. She regretted it now.

"Yeah, that's me," she said, hunkering down defensively.

"It's your fault I'm taking her to Paris for her birthday," he said, jovially, in spite of the complete discord with his stern face. "Great, she'll want a cruise next. You're going to bankrupt me."

"Sorry about that," Keira mumbled.

She gazed out the window, trying to switch her focus from the somewhat awkward conversation to the sight of a new, foreign city passing her by.

Berlin was stunning. Keira had heard about the city reinventing itself and moving on from its troubled history, but she hadn't expected it to be quite this vibrant and artsy. It seemed very youthful and cosmopolitan, like the quirkier parts of New York exemplified.

Her driver must have noticed her staring, because he said, "We'll be passing by a part of the wall soon."

Keira hadn't been sure whether she'd get a glimpse of the wall that had once divided East and West Berlin, splitting families apart and cleaving the city by political affiliation. She shuddered now as it came into view, a crumbled relic that the German people had torn down with their very hands. Mallory had watched the momentous occasion on the news, and it was a moment of triumph in history she seemed privileged to have witnessed. Keira felt humbled by the sight of it and took a photo with her cell phone in order to show Mallory when they were reunited at Christmas.

The cab carried on, drawing closer to the harbor. Keira caught sight of the ship even while they were still some distance away. It was huge, a gleaming white monstrosity. Her stomach fluttered with excitement.

Her driver pulled in to the drop-off spot. Keira took some euros from the envelope provided by Heather and handed them over his shoulder.

"Tell your wife hi from me," she said, feeling a little strange to be saying it.

"Enjoy your cruise," he replied in his incongruously warm voice and blank face.

Keira collected her case from the trunk and stared up at the enormous ship that was to be her home for the next fifteen days.

37

She took a deep breath to quell her excited butterflies, then headed confidently toward it.

*

The cruise ship was so much more beautiful than Keira had expected. Inside, it was decorated in an Art Deco style, with rich colors, bold geometric shapes, and ornaments. And even better than the unexpected glitz and glamour was the lavishness of a swimming pool and Jacuzzi on deck! Keira hadn't expected such luxury. She was going to love making this ship her home.

Filled with awe, she ventured to the bow, where there was a route all the way to the tip of the ship. It was impossible not to think of Jack and Rose on the *Titanic*, although she knew there was no love story in store for her, and she prayed there would be no icebergs either!

After a whistle-stop glance at the top deck, Keira went in search of her room. She'd been expecting to venture below deck, but to her surprise, her cabin was actually on the top deck. She found the door and went inside.

There was a round window, a proper brass-rimmed one like from a movie, and the view was straight out onto the ocean. Keira had been half expecting a cheap room, a little cubbyhole near the kitchens that smelled of food and was always noisy, but this was the opposite. Quiet, cozy, luxurious.

Her bed was made of chestnut wood, varnished so that it gleamed, and there were creamy silk sheets on it. On one of the small side tables was a silver bucket filled with ice and a bottle of champagne. She wondered who at the magazine had arranged that. Elliot wouldn't think to be so kind, and Heather would hate the extra, unnecessary expense. She wondered then if Nina had had a hand in it. They hadn't been on the best of terms since the furor over the Paris trip, where Nina had become so over-focused on the outcome she'd forgotten that Keira was a person with thoughts and feelings. But then she saw that there was a small card beside the champagne bucket. She picked up the card and opened it.

Welcome aboard, Keira Swanson! May I take this opportunity to express our deepest gratitude that your magazine has chosen our cruise company for your latest article. We are huge fans of Viatorum *and can't wait to be featured in your next issue.*

Keira stopped reading, discarding the card. The champagne wasn't from one of her caring work colleagues at all, but from the cruise company, attempting to butter her up so she'd write good things about them. Was the whole tour some kind of promotional thing? Some corporate back-scratching?

She grabbed her phone and texted Nina.

Is the cruise company advertising with us?

Nina replied quickly.

They're funding the trip. I assumed Elliot would have told you that.

Keira sighed. So the article was just basically a huge advertisement? It would've been nice to have been told in advance. At least that explained why Elliot had just plowed ahead and booked the trip without getting her final consultation as he'd promised last time around. Keira didn't want to sound like a spoiled brat, but *Viatorum* messed her around quite a lot. They certainly seemed to expect more from her than she did from them.

She sent another text to Nina.

How am I supposed to write about the cruise ship? A ship isn't a country.

When Nina texted back, her response shocked her.

You're not writing the next Great American Novel here. This isn't On the Road. Just say something nice so we all get paid.

Keira pouted and put her phone away. Nina was in a mood. Again. She didn't want it to spoil her enjoyment, so she pushed her irritation to the back of her mind.

Just then there was a knock on the door. Keira frowned and opened it. Standing outside was a young man dressed like a hotel bellboy. Keira immediately realized he was some kind of delegate from the cruise company, here to sweet-talk her. She really didn't feel like listening to the spiel.

"Hi, I'm Vince," he said, smiling and holding out a hand. Keira shook it despondently. "I've come to give you some brochures for our ship," he continued. "The *Revontulet,* which is the Finnish term for the Northern Lights."

Keira felt her smile return. She was excited to know in just a few days' time she'd be witnessing the infamous light display!

She took the brochures from Vince, feeling her mood improve considerably.

"Thanks. And for the champagne, too. It was a nice touch."

Vince nodded, his little hat bobbing as he did. "Your minibar is also stocked with liquors and snacks, all complimentary, of course."

Keira smirked. They were going to buy her affection through her stomach. It was quite a good strategy, she had to admit.

Vince hovered at the door. "If you'd like to be given a tour I can come back at a convenient time to show you all the facilities."

"I'm good," Keira said, declining. "I prefer to explore on my own terms." She held up the brochures he'd given her. "Besides, I've got all the info I need in here."

"Okay. If there's anything you need, just come to the information desk and ask for Vince."

"Will do," Keira said, knowing that she most definitely would not.

She shut the door and started to look through the brochure. Inside were all the details of things to do onboard the ship; there were comedy shows, live music events, karaoke, dances, even a cinema! She wouldn't be short on events to distract herself with, she thought wryly. Procrastination aboard the *Revontulet* might be hard to fight.

Then her stomach growled, reminding her that a diet of airplane food was hardly sufficient to get her through the day. She found the information on food. Dinner would be served in the main dining room. Again, she couldn't help but think of the *Titanic*.

It dawned on Keira then that she had no one to eat with. No tour guide this time, no one to discuss things with or bounce ideas off of. Eating alone had to be one of the loneliest activities in the world. She could always try video calling Bryn or one of her friends, but that would probably look a bit odd.

She decided then that instead of a lonely sit-down dinner, she'd spend the first evening aboard the *Revontulet* on the top deck, munching through some minibar snacks and drinking champagne. The company was footing the bill after all, so she ought to do what she wanted and what made her happy while she was here. It seemed like a much more enjoyable way to spend her time, she decided.

She looked through the little fridge, taking out a selection of foods, then grabbed the cool bottle of champagne. Drips ran down the sides and fell to the carpet as she left her room and headed for the deck.

On the port side of the boat were a series of sun loungers. Despite the evening weather, half of them were already occupied with lone travelers who'd had more or less the same idea as Keira. She selected one, laying her snacks out before her and placing the champagne bottle onto the table beside her.

As she settled in, the boat began to move. The sensation was bizarre, a sort of lurching undulation unlike anything her body had ever experienced before. Thinking now was as good a time as any, she grabbed her champagne bottle and popped the cork. Then, realizing she'd forgotten to take the cup from her room, she shrugged and took a swig straight from the bottle. Classy? No. But she didn't care.

She looked over her shoulder as Berlin began to grow smaller, its lights turning into little more than twinkling stars. Then she turned the other way and looked out at the blackness, at the ocean and dark sky, filled with excitement. She raised her glass to the air, toasting herself, her independence, and toasting the trip and all the new possibilities that lay ahead of her.

CHAPTER EIGHT

Slightly tipsy from the champagne, Keira felt her stomach begin to complain. Minibar food and plane food might have been sufficient for sober Keira, but tipsy Keira was ravenous. Plus, the bubbles made her bolder, and so she headed toward the dining room for dinner alone.

The dining room was as opulent as the rest of the ship, Art Deco as well. There was hardly anyone here at this time of evening, since it was approaching ten p.m. now. Keira followed a server to a small table that was positioned right beside the huge glass windows, affording her a wonderful view out to the open decks and the ocean beyond. She scanned the menu, pleased that it was written in English. She didn't feel like accidentally eating anything as exotic as the things Cristiano had in France!

It did feel very strange sitting alone. She had become accustomed to looking up from her menu and seeing Cristiano's gorgeous face. But no, not now, and she refused to get upset about it. She'd toasted her future, after all. It was all about being bold and independent now.

Although… it *had* been a long time since she'd spoken to Shane. She wondered how the family was since his father had passed. There was no Cristiano to glare jealously at her anymore, or make her feel bad about caring about her other ex's tumult. Maybe she should get back in touch with him, see how he was doing…

Before she had a chance to get her cell phone out of her bag, Keira became very aware of the sensation of eyes upon her. She turned her head and saw a woman at a nearby table quickly look away. She frowned and turned back to her table. Distracted from whatever it was she'd been about to do, she began to peruse her menu again.

The server returned then, taking Keira's order of a salted beef sandwich, fries, and Coke, before heading away. Keira followed his trajectory, looking over her shoulder to see whether she was still being observed by the woman. She was.

Her heart started to hammer then. Was it because she was alone? Way to make her feel worse about it, Keira thought. Surely people did this all the time, dining alone, being brave and

42

independent. She couldn't be the first person in the world that lady had ever seen eating dinner in her own company!

Her food arrived, and Keira ate with purpose, her ears burning from the sensation of being watched. She wondered whether everyone was looking at her with such judgment. But whenever she glanced about her at the few other diners they were all occupied with themselves, their own companions, their conversation, and their food. Only the middle-aged woman behind her seemed to be staring.

Keira grew more and more frustrated as she ate, formulating rebukes in her head for the woman along the lines of "Did no one ever teach you it's rude to stare?" As her fries diminished, she worked herself up into something of a frenzy, gearing herself up to go over and say something. When her plate was empty, she turned to discover the woman had gone. The moment had passed.

So it was with great alarm she turned back to her table and discovered the woman standing over her. Keira squealed loudly.

"Sorry!" the woman said, holding her hands up. She had a Texan accent. "I didn't mean to scare you!"

She was blond, with a heart-shaped face and delicate features.

"Where did you come from?" Keira exclaimed, looking around her, her heart racing with shock.

"I was just watching you all through dinner because I recognized your face," the woman admitted.

She was blushing suddenly. She pulled something from her purse and handed it to Keira. To Keira's surprise she was looking at an image of herself, in black and white, looking like a film star. And there was Cristiano. It was the front cover of *Viatorum*. The Paris issue.

"Oh," Keira said, feeling a strange sense of loss over the sight of the image.

"It is you, isn't it?" the woman asked hopefully.

"Yeah," Keira replied, sounding glum. "That's me."

The woman clapped her hands. "I knew it! I knew it! None of my friends believed me." She pointed to the bar, where the rest of her party had moved after vacating the dining table, and gave the four other women watching a thumbs-up.

The whole thing felt extremely odd to Keira. First Meredith in the office, then the taxi driver, and now this woman. She was becoming recognizable, something that, as a writer, she'd never really wanted to be! She knew she shouldn't have taken the cover image. It was so mortifying to be recognized from that silly, fantastical image rather than the more sensible one in her by-line!

"Hey, we're here on a bachelorette party," the woman told her. She was smiling broadly—not in a stalkerish way, Keira realized, but in an actually friendly way. "I don't suppose you'd want to join us?"

Keira felt too strange about the whole thing to join them, even though she was feeling even more lonely now that she'd been confronted with the image of Cristiano.

"I'd better not," she said. "I'm here on an assignment so I need to get an early night."

"You're writing an article?" the woman asked. "About the cruise?"

Her eyes seemed to be sparkling suddenly. It dawned on Keira then why. This woman must assume she was on the cruise *with* Cristiano, to write about their wonderful experience of being in love, of exploring the globe together. Only that was the opposite of what she was here to do.

"He's not onboard, by the way," Keira told her. "Cristiano, I mean. Sorry to dash your hopes, but it's just me."

The woman let out an exhalation. She looked disappointed. "He's not? But why?"

Keira plucked the tablecloth, her gaze focused on its strange design. "We broke up."

When she looked back up at the woman, her mouth was hanging open. Keira thought she even saw tears glittering in her eyes.

"But why?" the woman asked in a pained voice.

"It just didn't work out," Keira said, hurriedly.

Suddenly, she wanted to get away. To get far from her *fan* with her probing questions and staring eyes. She felt like some kind of specimen being studied under a microscope, an alien for people to gape at.

"Excuse me," she said, standing and discarding her napkin. "I'd better get some sleep. Nice to meet you."

She hurried away before the woman had a chance to say anything else.

CHAPTER NINE

Keira woke the next morning more than ready for a fresh start. So much for being bold and independent; her meeting with the reader yesterday had knocked her for a loop. But now, after a proper night's sleep in her luxurious bed, she was ready once more to face her task head on.

She washed in the small but comfortable en suite bathroom, then dressed for the day in casual faded denim jeans, black shirt and dark green woolen cardigan, finishing off her look with black, heeled ankle boots and some choice pieces of simple jewelry. Despite the gentle lulling motion of the ship, she managed to apply her makeup without any mishaps, opting for a natural but classy look. Then she tied her hair into a messy bun and felt ready to confront the day.

Keira left her cabin, locking the door behind her, and walked the length of the corridor toward the front of the ship. The dining room where breakfast was being served was right at the front of the ship, in order to have the most exciting views. She passed through the double glass doors into the room she'd only been dimly aware of through last night's haze of champagne. It looked different in the morning light, a little less decadent, and nowhere near as intimidating. Plus it was filled with guests eating their breakfasts, and the smell of fried eggs and bacon had never exactly been indicative of class.

Keira joined the small queue of waiting guests, and then a smartly dressed server showed her to a table. Not by the window this time, but in the corner, tucked away, just as Keira liked it. Still, she scanned the room to see whether the bachelorette party from yesterday was anywhere to be seen. Thankfully, they were not.

Keira took her laptop and notebook from her purse. She always laid the notebook out beside her in her moments of respite. Be it on a park bench in Paris or the breakfast table of a cruise ship, one never knew when the muse would strike. Unfortunately, the moment definitely didn't seem to be now. She needed to get some words over to Elliot and Nina but nothing was particularly forthcoming. She hoped that once they made their first destination she'd feel more inspired.

45

She became aware of a figure approaching and looked up to see a waiter coming over. He was a young man—she guessed late teens, twenty at a stretch—with dark auburn hair and freckles over every inch of his skin. He had warm hazel-colored eyes and perfectly aligned teeth which he flashed in a wide grin.

"Good morning," he said, eyeing her laptop as if trying to formulate something to say about it. "Have you decided what you're having for breakfast?"

Keira thought about the extra layer of flab around her stomach. "A coffee, please," she said.

The server nodded, but didn't leave. He must have been expecting her to order some food. Keira smiled in a way that she hoped suggested finality but he didn't get the hint.

"That's it," she added. "Just coffee. Nothing else."

He didn't move.

"So what are you writing?" he asked. "Are you an author? Or... no... a poet?"

Keira wasn't much in the mood for conversation. But she didn't want to be rude, so she replied simply, "Travel writer."

His eyes widened with interest. "No way. Are you writing about us? The cruise ship?"

"Not the ship per se," Keira replied. "But the destinations we visit, yes."

Her fingers went to the keyboard of her laptop, in what she hoped he'd take as an *I'm-busy* gesture. He did not.

"Awesome. Will you write about me?" He grinned and batted his eyelids.

Keira got the distinct impression then that this barely out of high school man-child was hitting on her. She felt a groan deep in the pit of her stomach.

"That depends," she said, looking up and smiling sarcastically. "On whether the coffee is any good."

He smirked. "A challenge. I like it. Well, I'm determined to fix you up the best coffee you've ever had in your life."

Keira folded her arms and drummed her fingers against them impatiently. "I'm deducting points for the time it's taking to arrive..."

He laughed then, clearly in no way concerned about delaying her caffeine fix, but he did at least retreat to fetch it for her.

Keira turned back to her screen and quickly typed.

If the only men who hit on me during this cruise are like my waiter, I'll pass the romance abstinence test with flying colors...

The waiter returned, a mug of coffee in hand. He placed it in front of her with a flourish. She saw in the cream he'd made the design of a heart. She rolled her eyes.

"Really?" she said dryly. "A heart?"

"A man's got to try," he replied, wiggling his eyebrows. "So? How did I do? Did I make the article?"

Keira reached for the mug and took a sip. "Oh yes," she said in a deadpan voice. "You made the article."

He punched the air as he walked away, and Keira smirked to herself. Little did he know!

*

Keira finished her breakfast and went up to the deck to watch the approaching landmass of Denmark. They'd been at sea for many hours and Keira felt excited at the prospect of standing on flat ground again.

She watched on as the boat slowed and pulled into the harbor of Copenhagen. It was such a beautiful, awe-inspiring experience, to see a city from the ocean first. Usually the first thing she saw of a new country was its airport, which quite frankly looked more or less the same as the one she'd taken off from. But this way the first sight her eyes beheld was a market stall–lined road and a row of terraced houses painted rainbow colors. It was far more magical.

As the ship's crew moored up, Keira headed off deck and to her cabin to collect a few more things for the day ahead. She went inside her room and picked up Heather's itinerary as well as the pamphlet on Denmark that the cruise company had left on her bedside table, along with pamphlets for the other locations she'd be visiting. She was about to leave when she decided to swap to a warmer jacket. The temperature was bound to be very chilly.

Then she headed back out, following rows of people all heading for the place where they could disembark. She flicked through the pamphlet. The ship was only stopping in Copenhagen for two days so she'd have to pick her day's activities wisely.

She decided her first stop would be Thorvaldsen's museum. She always enjoyed a healthy dose of art and culture before lunch, and the museum was exclusively for the sculptures of Danish artist Bertel Thorvaldsen. Then she'd stop for food before walking on to another museum, the Ny Carlsberg Glyptotek, to fill up on yet more art. Finally, she'd peruse the attached winter gardens to (hopefully) kick-start some nature-induced inspiration.

Keira filed off the boat, taking a deep breath of the fresh Danish air. The weather was as crisp as she'd anticipated and she wrapped her arms about her middle, grateful for the last-minute switch of jackets.

She began walking, idly at first, not too concerned with what direction she was heading but just glad to be on flat ground, and taking in the sights of a new foreign land. She wanted to really take some time to absorb the locale, to not taint her initial impressions of the city.

For the sake of exploration, she turned away from the harbor and headed along a cobblestone road lined with tall buildings, noting how bicycles seemed to outnumber cars two to one. The road led her to a vast tiled square with a fountain in the middle, a sight she felt was now synonymous with European cities. A busker played classical guitar in the center, and a small crowd of people placed coins in his upturned hat as they passed. So far so quaint, Keira thought.

She noticed a sign indicating the museum wasn't far, and so she decided to follow the directions to her first destination.

After she had negotiated several roads, the museum appeared before her. It was a large rectangular building painted vibrant orange, raised above ground level by a series of stone steps. There were five enormous doorways and an intriguing sculpture on the roof, which looked to Keira like horses pulling a chariot. People milled around outside, on the steps and surrounding square. She hurried inside, excited to see Bertel Thorvaldsen's sculptures in the flesh.

Inside, there was a very large corridor, with a domed ceiling, as well as the usual reception area to pay. Keira noticed a small group of people forming and realized that a tour was just about to take place.

"May I join the tour?" she asked the woman at the reception desk as she paid for her ticket.

"Yes," she replied, smiling. "You're just in time."

The woman handed Keira her ticket and she thanked her before heading toward the group, which mainly consisted of Japanese tourists. She slipped in amongst them and dug her notebook and pen from her bag.

The tour began, leading them through the first corridor of the marvelous building. The floor consisted of patterned tiles of interlocking geometric shapes, and the ceiling was a gorgeous, vibrant blue color. One side of the hallway consisted of windows, and lined along the inner wall were amazing sculptures of warriors.

"Over here," the tour guide said, "is the infamous *Cupid and Psyche* sculpture."

He led the group to the podium upon which the statue stood. Keira gazed up at the two figures, arm in arm, one a naked male, the other an androgynous figure with a swathe of fabric wrapped around their waist and stretching to their feet.

The tour guide began to explain the art to the group.

"Thorvaldsen was commissioned to make this sculpture, which depicts Psyche and Cupid, a popular subject at the time. Their story, if you're not familiar, is one of deep, true love. Cupid, the God of desire, eroticism, love, and attraction, was instructed by his mother, Venus, the goddess of beauty, to poison Psyche, whose immense beauty was eclipsing hers. But Cupid, on setting eyes upon Psyche, fell for her charms. Instead of cursing her to fall in love with a hideous serpent creature, he took her to his castle and made her his wife."

Keira rolled her eyes. She was so not in the mood to hear fantastical tales of immortal love and magic, knowing as she did that no such love truly existed.

The guide continued. "Incensed, Venus then sent Psyche on a series of quests, each one more torturous than the last. The final quest culminates in Psyche falling into an eternal sleep. And yet when Cupid finally tracks down his long-lost wife, he is able to bring her back to life." The guide finished his story with a triumphant, theatrical flourish. "The love they shared was so powerful it transcended even death."

Keira couldn't help herself. She scoffed aloud.

Suddenly, everyone fell silent. Keira looked up and saw the tour guide and the entirety of the tour group were now glaring at her. Everyone had heard her noise of disapproval.

Mortification overcame Keira. Her cheeks flushed pink. She hadn't meant to offend the guide in any way, she just thought the story of true love was silly. Now she felt awful.

"Sorry," she murmured.

The tour guide's face remained dark and unimpressed. Awkwardly, Keira slipped away from the rest of the group, consumed by embarrassment.

*

Keira's cheeks were still burning when she stopped in the first cute cafe she could find. It was a bit early for lunch, but she ordered coffee and a sandwich nonetheless, then went and sat at a table in the window, looking out at the world passing her by.

Copenhagen was very pretty to look at, and the gray skies did little to diminish its charm. Most of the buildings were painted in bright colors, which certainly helped, and the throngs of tourists always present in a capital city added to the cheery atmosphere. And yet, her trusty notebook—lying out on the table beside her as always—was still empty.

She attempted to write some initial lines and impressions of Copenhagen.

Quaint. Charming.

Then she sighed and gave up. Nothing was forthcoming. Her writer's block was particularly acute at the moment, thanks in no doubt to her sadness over the breakup.

She concentrated instead on eating her food and getting on with her day. Eating alone still wasn't a particularly enjoyable experience, and it made her uncomfortable sitting here surrounded by groups of people and couples having a lovely time. With Cristiano, breakfast, lunch, and dinner had been exciting events, but on her own, eating was just a means to an end. She didn't even want to try any of the strange local dishes, like the unpronounceable smørrebrød or spegepølse. She just wanted it to end as quickly as possible.

As soon as she'd eaten, she headed back out into the streets.

Following the signposts to the Ny Calsberg museum, Keira discovered she was approaching a giant glass house. She went inside, into what was known as the winter gardens, and was taken aback by how breathtakingly beautiful it was, with huge trees brushing the glass ceiling above her. The smell of fresh vegetation was intoxicating. She could imagine the winter gardens being the perfect location for a proposal or wedding ceremony. It felt magical and very romantic, two words she jotted down in her notebook.

After touring the gardens she went inside to look at the artwork and all the different sculptures. She noticed a young couple looking entranced by it all. For the first time since starting her trip, she felt the urge to speak to someone new. She went up to them, taking her notebook from her purse as she went.

"I'm so sorry to interrupt," she said to the woman, a tall, natural blond with icy blue eyes.

The girl smiled genially. "Can I help?"

"I'm a travel writer," Keira explained, holding up her notebook as some kind of proof to her claim. "I was wondering if I could speak to you about Copenhagen."

"Oh," the boy said this time. "We're not local, though."

"That's okay," Keira replied. "I'm just interested in your experiences of the city. How has it been for you so far?"

The young couple looked at each other, flashing glances that communicated their deep love and affection.

"It's been wonderful." The girl smiled.

The boy nodded his agreement.

"What's been your highlight?" Keira asked.

The couple shared another glance.

"For me, the walking bridge," the girl said. "Where lovers write their names on padlocks."

"Oh yes," Keira replied, scribbling it down quickly. A lover's bridge seemed to be another staple of European cities. "Anything a bit more Copenhagen specific?"

"The *Little Mermaid* statue," the boy suggested.

Of course, Keira thought. The most famous Danish love story. She could use the tragedy of the Little Mermaid (the Hans Christian Andersen original version, not the cartoon one!) as a springboard for her article.

"Great, I'll visit that," she said, jotting it down so as not to forget.

The couple headed off, hand in hand, almost as if they'd already forgotten their brief interview with Keira, with eyes only for each other. Keira watched them go with a pang of longing in her chest.

She checked the time and realized that thanks to having cut off the museum tour early and scarfing her lunch down, she still had plenty of time for another attraction before returning to the ship for dinner. She took out her pamphlet, considering castles and museums, until she saw something that really caught her attention. The Fredericksberg Rundell ice rink. Getting a bit of physical exercise would certainly be a welcome change from feeling lonely in museums and cafes.

It took over half an hour to walk to the ice rink but Keira didn't mind, since it gave her the opportunity to see more of the city. Besides, it was very pedestrian friendly, with hardly any cars and many pedestrianized areas, the old roads paved over and now home to awesome spruce trees. The city was really made for walking, Keira thought, as she took a deep, calming breath.

When she arrived at the Fredericksberg Rundell ice rink, it was amazing, not to mention huge. Keira hired skates and joined the throngs of people. Whizzing around was exhilarating. For the first time in a while, she felt like she was really doing something for herself. She realized then that she was having *fun,* even though she was on her own. Her desire for independence was finally starting to come true.

*

Keira returned to the boat, taking up her spot on the sun lounger on the deck as she had the night before, only this time without the champagne. It was very peaceful out on deck, with the sound of the ocean sloshing against the sides of the boat and a million stars above her.

She got out her notebook and began to write a few snippets from her day, of her faux pas during the museum tour, and the couple she'd met in the winter gardens, and the exhilaration she'd felt during the solo ice skating. She read it back, pleased but instinctively knowing that *Viatorum* would hate it. It read far too much like a diary entry rather than that delicate balance between travel and romance she'd found in her previous work.

Just then, Keira's phone started ringing. She jumped. It had felt like a long time since she'd properly spoken to anyone, and the moment she thought it she realized it was true. She hadn't really had a full conversation all day.

She looked at the name flashing on the screen and was shocked to discover that it was Cristiano. She stared at her phone in her hand, deliberating over what to do. Today had been the first day she'd felt good on her own. She didn't want to spoil that newfound freedom by hearing Cristiano's voice. And besides, that stupid text message she'd sent still remained unspoken between them. She was far too embarrassed to even broach the subject with him.

By the time she'd decided not to answer the call, the phone had stopped ringing. She waited for a moment to see if he would leave a voicemail. But none came.

Keira felt a pang of loneliness. She realized then that this was exactly what her boss and editor would want to know about; the longing, the fighting against her own instincts to find someone new who could soothe the pain. Once again, she'd need to put her heart on the line and lay out all her vulnerabilities for the world to see. As the Romance Guru, her heartbreak was in demand.

She sighed, sadly, and began to write.

CHAPTER TEN

Keira had just one more day in Denmark, one day to conjure up some words to send to the magazine. She hadn't yet found her groove with this article. Maybe some more interviews would help.

She dressed herself for the day, then went to the dining hall for breakfast. As she entered she saw that the ginger-haired server from before was on shift again. She groaned internally in anticipation of his flirty ways. Except, when he came up to show her to a spare table, he seemed morose. He greeted her with a simple "Good morning" and quietly led her to her table. No flirty quips whatsoever.

Keira sat, looking up at him curiously. He handed her a menu with an audible sigh.

"Is everything okay?" Keira asked.

"Yeah," he said dismissively and wholly unconvincingly. "What are you having? Coffee again?"

Keira nodded. "And oatmeal. Thanks."

He wandered away. She watched him go.

She took her notebook out, glancing back over the few scribbled passages she'd written of her first impressions of Copenhagen. There weren't many, just the embarrassing experience at the museum and the brief interview with the loved up tourists in the winter gardens. At least she could call the Denmark leg of her journey a success in terms of not rebounding. She'd barely spoken to anyone, let alone had the chance to fall in love.

Just then, her server returned with her breakfast. He placed it on the table before her, eyeing the notebook in her hands.

"How's it going?" he asked. "The article, I mean."

His tone was so completely different from how it had been the last time they'd met that Keira couldn't help but worry. He seemed thoroughly depressed.

"Not great," she admitted. "I haven't interviewed enough people." Suddenly, Keira had an idea. "Hey, how about I interview you?" she asked.

The server raised both his ginger eyebrows. "Me?"

"Sure," she replied, smiling kindly. He looked like he was in desperate need of human contact, or, at the very least, something to distract him from his unhappiness. "It's not exactly busy this morning. Why don't you take a seat?" She gestured to the chair opposite.

The server looked over his shoulder at the more or less empty dining room. He wasn't the only person on shift. Finally, he shrugged and took a seat.

"What do you want to know?" he asked.

"Well," Keira began, picking up her coffee mug and taking a small sip. "My articles are always romance themed. I travel abroad and talk to locals about what love is like where they're from." She decided to omit the part about falling in love herself—she didn't want to give him any ideas! "It's been tricky this time as I'm only passing through Denmark for a few days. So far I've just been rubbing shoulders with tourists."

"I can't help you there," he replied. "I'm not from Denmark."

"No," she agreed, having already noted his British accent. "But you *can* give me an insight into what it's like being on a cruise ship. Since the ship is going to be the one constant during my entire trip, it might make sense for me to frame the story around it."

"This sounds very complicated for a travel article," he quipped.

"Tell me about it," Keira replied, wryly. "I'd much prefer to be a travel food writer. Have my own spin-off TV show. A blog. A book." She looked wistfully away. Then she shook her head and turned back to the ginger-haired boy in front of her. "But one step at a time. Anyway, back to you."

The boy's eyes fell to the table top. "Me? Well, honestly, I don't have any luck in love whatsoever. I'm on here for months at a time. There was a singer last summer, she was lovely. But there's always a time limit. A month or two, then they're off on another boat, in another part of the world."

Keira swallowed the spoonful of oatmeal she'd been eating as he spoke. "Where is she now? The singer?"

"The Caribbean," he said, sighing. "Having a mad love affair with the double bass player." He took his cell phone out of his pocket and scrolled through some pictures, then held it out to Keira. "See?"

She looked at the image of a beautiful young girl in a sparkly red dress smiling broadly beside a handsome man in a suit.

"She's pretty," Keira commented. "How old is she?"

"Nineteen, like me," he said, sighing again. "I shouldn't follow her on social media, really. Every season she finds a new guy. Every season it breaks my heart all over again."

"I'm sorry," Keira said, empathetically. "That must be hard."

She studied the photo again, and couldn't help but think the singer's story resonated so much with her own. While Keira had a different country and tour guide, this singer had a different cruise ship and crew. Except she looked a ton happier about it than Keira was!

Was age the difference? Keira wondered. That transitory, nomadic lifestyle lent itself more favorably to younger people, straight out of college, who wanted to have as many new experiences as possible, who had all the time in the world to find true love.

Or maybe it wasn't age at all, but attitude. What if she'd been approaching the Romance Guru assignments all wrong? Before she'd landed this gig, she'd been doing the whole stable relationship routine with Zach, and ever since then she'd attempted to replicate that. With Shane. With Cristiano. But it was never going to work because the circumstances underpinning those relationships were entirely incompatible with, well, *relationships*. She'd been trying to find *love,* following society's (and Mallory's) demand that she should settle down now that she was fast approaching her thirties. But that was never going to work! She should be falling in lust. She should be collecting experiences just like the broadly smiling singer in the photograph. She'd never had the chance to do it in her early twenties because she'd been so focused on her career, and then Zach came along and it was safe and easy not to think about it.

The answer hit her then, so forcefully it was like a lightning bolt. She was getting so hurt because she was confusing lust and love. Well, no more!

She snapped her notebook shut. She knew exactly how she was going to frame her article now.

The server jumped with surprise.

"Thank you," she said, grinning. "You've really helped me."

"I have?" he asked, looking confused.

"Yup," she said. She stood, slinging her notebook back into her bag. She took a final sip of coffee, then bent down and kissed the server's freckled cheek. "Have a nice day," she said, breezily.

Then she left, leaving the bemused server at her table.

*

Keira practically skipped to the walking bridge. Her mind was full of inspiration, at last. The Romance Guru had had a breakthrough and she couldn't wait to share it with her readers.

Her readers.

The thought repeated in her mind, making her stomach leap with pleasure. How amazing to think that she now had an audience, that people cared about what she had to say, that she entertained and advised and supported other women just like herself. And that they in turn supported her, helping her make each small step towards independence and greater self-awareness. She grinned to herself.

The bridge appeared ahead of her and Keira saw that it was rammed with couples and covered in locks. She grabbed her notebook and beelined toward the first couple who looked local.

"*Hej!*" she said, smiling. "*Taler du Engelsk?*"

"Yes," the man said. Like everyone Keira had seen in Denmark, he was exceptionally tall and wearing a bobble hat. "We speak English. Are you looking for something? We can give you directions."

"Actually I'm a writer working on an article about love. I was wondering if I could interview you and your lovely partner here." She gestured to the woman beside him, who was also very tall, and also in a bobble hat.

"Sure," he said.

"Great." Keira grinned. She flipped her notebook open. "So what brings you guys to the bridge today?"

"We're putting on a lock, of course," the woman said. She held up a huge gold lock that had two sets of initials drawn on it in thick, black pen, surrounded by a heart.

"And what does the lock symbolize for you?" Keira asked.

The woman pondered this for a long time. "Unity," she said finally.

"Are you married?" Keira asked.

"Nope," the woman replied.

"Are you planning on it?"

The woman looked up at her partner. "Nope. It's not such a big thing over here."

Keira frowned. "Marriage isn't a big thing? What do you mean?"

The man spoke next. "Our society is about egalitarianism. Equality between the genders. We have equal things like paternity and maternity leave, no pay gap between the genders, and a lot less marriage."

Keira scribbled everything down quickly. "Would you say, anecdotally speaking, that you have more relationships as a result? If people aren't marrying then what about commitment?"

"Probably," the woman replied. "People commit when they have kids, usually. That's the signifier over here, not marriage. If people have kids they tend to stick together at least until they've left home for uni. That's the contract, I would say."

The man nodded in agreement. "Yeah, I think so too. It's sort of like you're saying, okay, we're in this for at least twenty more years. But no one pretends it's going to be forever. It's illogical, don't you think?"

Keira thought about how their words built on what she'd been thinking over breakfast. This whole pressure to settle, to find The One; what if it just didn't work in modern society anymore? In the past people had so many fewer opportunities. The pool of mates was far smaller. People were expected to want to spend their twenties, thirties, forties, everything with the same person. One person was supposed to fulfill all their needs at every single one of their life stages. But the world didn't work that way now. Now it was far more common to spend a whole decade after college working on yourself, to leave kids until your thirties. But then you'd still be considered young at fifty when those kids went off on their own. How likely was it, really, that the person you were with at fifty would still be the one for the next forty years of your life!

"I think I'd have to agree," Keira replied, looking at the man. "Thanks, you've given me lots of food for thought."

She watched as the couple put their lock on the bridge, wondering whether it might end up being more permanent than their actual relationship.

Keira was struck by a sudden desire then to put her own lock on the bridge. Not for a relationship, though, but for some other reason. What would a lock symbolize for her? Her job? Her independence? Or just herself? That no matter who she spent time with, who she shared those milestones of her life with, she'd always have herself?

Just then, Keira overheard what sounded like an argument coming from a little way down the bridge. She stepped closer, curious.

The couple were speaking English, and she could tell they were tourists just by their shorter stature.

"I said I wanted the lock to be pink!" the woman was exclaiming. In her hands was an ordinary bronze lock, like the ones most people used. "It's not special if it's not pink!"

The man she was with looked flustered. "I couldn't get pink," he told her. "It's special because it's ours."

"It won't stand out!" she yelled back, gesturing at the wall of bronze locks, of which theirs would just be another of many. "Why can't you ever do anything I ask you to?"

The man looked hurt, crushed even, that what had clearly started as a romantic gesture had blown up into a public embarrassment.

The girl grabbed the lock from his hands then and threw it over the bridge. It plopped into the sea. Keira gasped.

The girl turned on her heel and stormed away, passing Keira in a flurry of anger. Everyone stared at her as she went. Her poor boyfriend just stood there, flabbergasted, watching her storm away. Then he suddenly returned to his senses.

"Bianca!" he yelled, hurrying past the crowds, his cheeks bright red. "Bianca, come back!"

Keira quickly wrote down the whole encounter. When she looked up again, there was a lock seller passing her pushing a wooden barrel. Every single lock in the barrel was pink. Keira laughed to herself, amused, and, without wasting a second, stopped the man pushing the barrel.

"Can I buy a lock please?" she asked.

"Of course," he said with a smile, taking out one of the pink locks and handing it to her. "You like pink?"

Keira smirked to herself. "It's my favorite color."

She paid for the lock, thoroughly amused. Then she looked at it in her hand. She wasn't sure what the lock would symbolize for her yet. But she knew that standing here, in Denmark, was a special experience and that putting a lock on the bridge would be like making her own mark. That she was doing it alone only made it more meaningful for her. It was a once in a lifetime opportunity.

She grabbed a Sharpie from her bag and wrote on the pink lock: The Romance Guru. Then she grinned to herself and locked it to the bridge.

CHAPTER ELEVEN

Keira checked her watch and saw there wasn't much time before the ship left the harbor, heading for its next destination. So she left the lover's bridge and headed to the harbor to see the *Little Mermaid* statue. It seemed even more appropriate to her now to see it.

The mermaid looked out to sea, waiting for her love to return, a lover she'd sacrificed everything for. Keira thought of herself, and the things she had sacrificed for men. For Zach, it had been love in general. They'd never really loved each other, but had bobbed happily along side by side for two whole years. Shane had taken from her her sense of wonder, because she knew she'd never recapture that feeling now of abandon, of throwing caution to the wind. That experience had left her jaded. Cristiano had taken more from her; a chunk of her heart was missing because of him, although she couldn't fully understand why. Whatever the reason, each of the men had made a deep mark on her. Each had taken a piece from her that she would never get back.

Her high from breakfast suddenly faded, as she looked upon the morose mermaid statue. The sense of loneliness etched into the stone features seemed to mirror her own. Love or lust, whatever it was, experiencing it too often was still emotionally taxing.

She glanced over then and saw a couple taking engagement photos nearby. They were taking a long time to perfect their pose, with the girl holding up a huge sparkling diamond as the man kissed her cheek. Keira watched them, taking shot after shot until finally they'd found the perfect one. How many false starts, how many attempts, did it take until it was perfect? Was it ever perfect or had they settled? Was that all that marriage really meant? Choosing not to experience the toll of lust, love, heartache, and heartbreak anymore? Finding someone else who'd had enough of it as well? Putting a big sparkly symbol on your finger that screamed to all nearby: This will do!

A melancholy came over her. She looked around, seeing couples, looking at them skeptically. What was it, really, that they were looking for and finding in each other?

Just like when she'd arrived in Denmark, Keira felt suddenly, agonizingly alone.

*

Keira wanted to watch the ship pulling out of the harbor so she went up on deck with a glass of wine and found her lounger. As she waited, the sky darkening around her, she wrote some notes about the day.

Her change in mood had been abrupt. It was amazing how the same thought—that there was no One, no single person that could fulfill your needs at all the different stages of life—could be empowering in one minute and crushingly painful the next. How she'd gone from laughing at the pink lock debacle, glad she wasn't in such a mess, to staring longingly at a couple taking engagement photos, wondering whether it would ever be her turn.

She hovered her pen over the paper, then wrote down one simple phrase:

My mind is a mess.

Sighing, Keira took a sip of wine. It was very cold tonight, and she wrapped her arms around her chest, drawing warmth from herself. Then she heard the engines change sound and knew that they'd be leaving Denmark soon.

She didn't know what to make of the place, or how to quantify her experience there. She hadn't fallen in love *or* lust, so she could chalk that up as a win. But how to express that in words, she couldn't work out.

She heard the churning noise of water then; propellers cutting through waves. The boat rumbled from friction, then started moving. Keira's stomach flipped from the sensation.

She watched Denmark shrink from view, until its lights were little more than a twinkle on the horizon. Out in the ocean, it was even colder. And as they picked up speed, the wind chill stung Keira's face. It was too much to bear, so she collected her notebook and wine and headed back inside to the comfort of her room.

She poured another glass of wine and settled at the desk, looking through the small round window at the empty expanse of ocean. There really was nothing like the sight of, well, *nothing,* to really heighten one's sense of loneliness.

Keira could bear it no more. She grabbed her cell phone and called Bryn.

"Hey, lil sis," her sister said as she answered. "How's Denmark?"

"A smudge on the horizon, thankfully," Keira told her.

"Oh?" Bryn said, quizzically. "You didn't like it?"

"The country? It was lovely. Like everywhere in Europe I've seen. Beautiful. Historic. Romantic. It's just that I'm alone and it's hard to have fun on your own, even if you are in a unique city like Copenhagen."

"Oh, sweetie," Bryn said, sounding empathetic.

Keira found it strange how much kinder Bryn was these days. Felix was having a great effect on her.

"How's everything with you?" Keira asked. "Did you move yet?"

"Pretty much," Bryn told her. The smile was audible in her voice. "We've sold some furniture, bought some stuff for the both of us, worked out some color schemes, that sort of thing."

"Full steam ahead," Keira said. "No pun intended."

Bryn laughed. "Enough about me," she said for what Keira was certain was the first time in her life ever. "How are you? You sound really down."

"I am," Keira said with a deep sigh. "I mean, I'm kind of up and down, you know. Apt considering the waves are literally moving me up and down." She chuckled sadly to herself. "But I had, like, an epiphany this morning and I was really motivated. But by the afternoon it was completely gone and suddenly I felt awful again. All this focus on love is draining."

She paused, realizing Bryn hadn't even interrupted her. It was like her sister had had a brain transplant. Not that Bryn was usually awful, but she usually had a lot to say, an opinion she just had to express about everything. Keira wasn't used to being given the time and space to fully explain herself.

"You know, you're getting really good at listening," Keira told Bryn. But then, on the other end of the line, she heard nothing but silence. Assuming her sister was joking, she laughed. "Yes, yes, very funny."

But still, there was silence. Keira took her cell phone from her ear and discovered the call had disconnected. The bars that indicated how much signal she had were now empty. The call had cut out. She had no idea how long ago.

Keira sighed, sadly, and headed to bed.

CHAPTER TWELVE

Keira was woken the next morning by the sound of her cell phone ringing. The boat was rocking in a more pronounced manner than it had so far, and it made her stomach roll a little. She groaned, reached out, and grasped for her phone. It was the *Viatorum* office, which meant either Nina, Heather, or, on rare occasions, Elliot. She answered the call with anticipation.

"Keira, hi," came Nina's voice.

Keira let out a breath of relief. Nina was definitely her preference out of the three options.

Nina continued speaking. "Look, the article so far is fine. Your description of Denmark, your amusing story about the museum. But we need more." She paused. "More interaction. It's hardly a challenge not to rebound if you haven't given yourself the chance to actually meet anyone."

"Being a hermit crab is one way to make sure I don't fall in love," Keira joked.

Nina didn't seem to be in the joking mood. "Keira, come on. You know what we're looking for by now. This is your fourth assignment. I shouldn't need to be holding your hand."

Keira felt the sting of Nina's words. From Elliot, she wouldn't have cared so much, but Nina was supposed to be a friend first, co-worker second. She was starting to get a bit too big for her boots since she'd transitioned from an assistant editor—one of many—to just editor. Cream of the crop. In fact, Keira couldn't even recall the last time they'd actually socialized together outside of work. She sighed.

"I hear what you're saying," Keira said. "You want me to experience temptation, right? To get close enough for love but decide against it." Her voice was flat as she spoke. She understood the rules now. The game they wanted her to play.

"That would be a good start," Nina replied. "And a damn sight more interesting than this passage about a sad mermaid."

"The *Little Mermaid* statue," Keira replied between her teeth. "I thought that passage was poignant."

"Readers don't want poignant," Nina challenged. "They want to see you interact. They want to see you skulk away under the disapproving glare of a group of Japanese tourists because you've scoffed aloud at a story of love, not read about you wistfully comparing yourself to a statue. Get out and SPEAK to people, dammit."

"I can't today," Keira told Nina tersely. "I'm stuck on the boat. We won't reach Finland for another twenty-four hours."

The ocean waves swelled beneath her then in a sickening motion. Keira prayed there wouldn't be twenty-four more hours of this to get through.

"Then speak to someone on the cruise," came Nina's curt response. "The cruise is supposed to be part of the article too and you haven't said a thing about it, other than that tiny section about your server in the dining room. Interview some people. Go to a play. Meet a boy. Watch the entertainment on a date and come up with some lovely extended metaphor about love and the ocean."

"And what about Scandinavia?" Keira replied scathingly.

"Just add in some snow! Okay?"

Keira was stunned by Nina's attitude. It wasn't like her friend to pull rank on her like that. In fact, she was sounding more and more like Joshua every day! She started wondering whether Nina could even be classified as her friend anymore at all.

"Fine," she finally replied. "I'll write a passage about love on a ship, if it will please you."

Nina ended the call before Keira had a chance to say goodbye.

Peeved from the call and nauseous from the boat, Keira didn't exactly feel like hurrying to breakfast. Instead, she went into the adjacent bathroom and spent a long time soaking in the hot shower water, mulling everything over in her mind. *Viatorum* was starting to push and pull her around in all directions. Sometimes the way they treated her was flat out rude. In fact, Zachary of all people had been more polite to her recently than her employers had! A difficult conversation was going to have to take place when she returned home. She'd thought she'd gotten her point across to Elliot last time but clearly nothing had sunk in.

She left the shower room and sat on her vanity stool. Her image swayed in the reflection in front of her, rocking from left to right in syncopated rhythm. This was by far the worst day to be stuck onboard. The last thing she'd be able to do was enjoy the entertainment. The thought of a date made her toes curl. Perhaps this article was going to end up closer to fiction than fact.

She dried and styled her hair, put some "approachable" makeup on—neutral shades, nothing bold—and a "friendly" looking outfit—jeans, slogan T, flat shoes—then headed out of her room, locking the door behind her.

The corridor lurched from left to right, making her stumble. Getting to the breakfast bar took double the time as usual.

When she got there, she found her ginger-haired server at his wooden podium. His usually brown freckled skin was looking strangely green. He appeared to be holding himself up with the podium rather than standing beside it.

"Morning," he grumbled.

"Are you okay?" Keira asked. "You don't look well."

"Seasick," he said. "If I were you, I'd grab something and take it on deck. Watching the horizon and breathing fresh air is the only way to stop seasickness."

"Thanks for the tip," she replied.

She staggered over to the buffet area and took a bagel and little pot of cream cheese, then a bottle of water and an apple. So much for dieting…

"No coffee?" the server asked as she passed.

She shook her head. "I think it would make me sick."

"I think that's a good call," he replied, making a grim face. "I regret mine this morning."

She laughed and headed out to the deck.

The cold air hit her like a slap to the face. They were geographically further north now and the weather had chilled further to match. She found her now usual lounger, sat down, and began to munch on the bagel while looking through the ship's brochure of entertainment. There was a play on during the day, and after that a live band with dancing. Keira shrugged. There wasn't anything else to do so she may as well just go to both. A play wouldn't be particularly sociable but hopefully she'd use the time to get some inspiration and ideas for the extended metaphor Nina was after. Besides, the dance later on should make up for it. There'd be tons of people to talk to there.

She finished her breakfast and wiped the crumbs from her lap, then headed back inside the boat to find the theater. As the ship rocked her from side to side she tried to come up with some phrases for her article.

Now single, I'm standing on ground as unsteady as the deck beneath my feet.

She staggered down unfamiliar corridors, following the directions toward the entertainment deck, which she'd not yet visited. Maybe Nina had a bit of a point—though expressed badly. She *had* been extremely unsociable on this trip.

She wondered now why that was. She'd never considered herself a particularly shy person, but she wasn't as sociable as Bryn, or Maxine, say. She was just driven. There were a million other things she wanted to do more than chat. So why then was she so personable when it came to Shane? And Cristiano? Was she one of those women who only bothered to speak to people she could get something from? The thought troubled her.

At last, she made it to the entertainment deck and theater where the play was soon to take place. They'd made a whole song and dance of it, with staff dressed up like posh hotel porters, right down to the little hats. She went over to the one standing beside the door.

"Am I right in thinking there's a play taking place today?" she asked him.

"Yes. *Romeo and Juliet,*" he replied.

"Oh," Keira said.

Romeo and Juliet. The world's most romantic play. Immediately she was reminded of the Juliet balcony she'd visited on her prior assignment. When her heart and head had been in completely different places. When she had been a different person, unmarked by the recent changes and experiences of her life.

"Is that a problem?" the man said then, snapping her back to the moment. "You look devastated."

"Sorry," Keira said, coming back to the conversation. "It just has a bit of a personal significance to me." He looked at her quizzically, and she added, "I'm a writer. Romance travel articles. Bit niche, but basically I travel the world interviewing people about love."

"That sounds really interesting," the man replied. "Why don't you speak to some of the actors?"

Keira's eyes widened. "Do you think they'd want to speak to me?"

He gave her a look then. "They're actors. Speaking is literally their favorite thing to do. Want me to take you backstage?"

"That would be great!" Keira grinned.

The man opened the large entrance doors and beckoned her inside. The theater was just like a normal-looking theater, a big stage, a red velvet curtain, balconies. The only real difference was the way the chairs were bolted down to the floor.

Keira felt quite excited about this trip backstage. Imagine Nina's face when she read the next section of her article starring Romeo and Juliet, *the* Romeo and Juliet!

The corridors were dark and the movement of the ship made it even more disorientating. But at last they emerged into a brightly lit area which reminded Keira of a gym changing room. There, sitting in a chair in the corner, was a woman tapping into her cell phone dressed up in period clothes. Juliet, she guessed.

"That's Anita," the staff member said. "Juliet. And Romeo is over there." He pointed to where a shirtless man was doing pull-ups. "Dirk."

Romeo looked up at the intruders. "Can I help you?"

Keira looked to the staff member for some kind of support but he left the floor to her. She cleared her throat. "I'm a writer," she announced. "I write romance articles. I wondered if I could speak to you about your roles and love."

Juliet put her phone down. "Ooh, I'd love that!" she exclaimed, smiling.

She was incredibly beautiful, Keira noticed. And she had a Scandinavian accent. At last, a local!

Keira left Romeo to his workout and went over to Juliet, who patted the seat beside her, grinning invitingly.

"Hi!" the girl said, when Keira sat. She appeared much younger on closer inspection. "This is so cool. Am I going to be in a newspaper or something?"

"A magazine," Keira told her. "*Viatorum*."

Anita shrugged. "I've not heard of it. Sorry."

"That's okay," Keira replied. "We're relatively small. At the moment anyway. We're growing every day."

Anita smiled. "So how can I help you?"

"Basically, I travel the world and ask people about love, marriage, that sort of thing."

Anita rolled her eyes immediately. "I'm the least Juliet-like Juliet you'll ever meet," she said.

"You're another Scandi who hates marriage?"

"We don't hate it," she rebuked. "We just prefer partnerships, you know? Marriage is *so* patriarchal. No one really bothers here, or at least not until they're much older."

"How old is older?" Keira asked, writing Anita's words down.

"Like, late thirties."

Keira thought of her mom back in New York City, always telling her she needed to settle down soon, having children before her biological clock imploded. "What about starting families? Won't it be a bit risky to be leaving it until that age?"

Anita looked confused. "You don't need to be married to start a family. My parents weren't."

"Me neither," Dirk piped up from the other side of the room, mid pull-up. "They didn't marry until they were in their fifties."

"And that's common?" Keira asked.

Both Romeo and Juliet shrugged.

"Guess so," Anita said. "Maybe not common but certainly accepted."

"So you're in no hurry?"

"Nah," she said, sounding incredibly un-Juliet-like. "Are you?"

Keira pondered the question. Was she? She didn't even know what she wanted anymore. Her mind was scrambled when it came to matters of love.

"I don't think so," she admitted. "So tell me about partnerships then, rather than relationships or marriage or anything like that. Do you find yourself wanting to cozy up with someone to beat the cold?"

"Sure." Anita grinned. "My dog. He's a husky!"

She turned her cell phone to show Keira an enormous snow-white husky with gorgeous blue eyes. Keira laughed.

"He's all I need to keep warm," Anita added.

Keira found her attitude extremely refreshing. A young woman with literally no concern about love, marriage, families, or anything of the like.

"You don't seem particularly interested in love, if you don't mind me saying," Keira told her.

"Ironic, huh?" Anita replied. "Considering my job." She gestured to her Juliet robe. "But that's sort of why. My job is way more important to me."

Keira remembered the conversations she'd had with her red-haired server, about his lover and her complete lack of desire for love, her priority and drive being experience, work, *life*.

Just then, a voice sounded over a PA system. "Fifteen minutes until curtain."

Anita looked apologetically at Keira. "I'd better get in the zone. Are you staying for the play?"

"I am," Keira said, folding her notebook up.

She was looking forward to it so much more now that she'd gotten to know a bit about Juliet.

"Cool," Anita said. "Stick around after and we can head to the party together if you want?"

"I'd love that," Keira replied, trying not to sound too eager. But Anita seemed like great, fun company and she was craving company right now. Not romantic company, she realized, but just friendship. It occurred to her then that her loneliness was as much about a desire for friends as it was about missing Cristiano.

She stood and headed back out into the black corridor. The boat was still swaying and she staggered a little, groping in the darkness. She tried to remember the way she'd come when she'd been following the cruise ship staff member, but it was impossible now. She guessed right and was relieved to hear the sound of a chattering crowd from nearby that indicated she was at least heading in the right direction. She turned in the direction she was certain would be the exit back into the theater.

Suddenly the boat lurched. She reached out to steady herself against what appeared to be a wall, and was surprised when her hands hit something that felt like heavy fabric, before going straight through them. She stumbled forward, losing her footing. She hit the hard ground and felt the air rush out of her. Suddenly, she became very aware of the sensation of eyes upon her. She looked up and discovered she'd fallen straight through the stage curtain and was now lying sprawled on the middle of the stage in front of a bemused-looking handful of cruise passengers. Her cheeks burned immediately.

She tried to collect herself up to her feet, but the boat kept rocking and she couldn't find her footing. The small group of people already in their seats waiting for the show to start started to giggle with amusement. Keira realized it was one of those can't-beat-'em situations and gave up, lying sprawled on her back, succumbing to laughter.

*

Keira wasn't sure why she'd been so reluctant to see the play (other than the obvious romantic subject matter), because it was actually outstanding. Anita was a wonderful actor, as was Dirk, who was almost unrecognizable when fully clothed. It was amazing to Keira that two people she'd met and casually chatted with backstage could possess such astounding talent.

As the curtain fell on the play, Keira found herself clapping along as rapturously as everyone else. And suddenly she was now really looking forward to her night ahead, spending a bit more time getting to know the pair, and picking their brains about the nuances of romantic life in the Scandinavian and the Nordic regions. She was already beginning to formulate the passage she'd write for this experience in her head, and felt the first twinkles of her creative muse.

As the audience filed out, Keira collected her things and headed for the theater bar where Anita would be meeting her once she'd changed out of her Juliet attire. She drew up to it, seeing that just a handful of people were lingering around there, most presumably heading off to some other cruise ship activity.

She took a stool and ordered red wine, then took out her notebook to jot down some notes during the time she had to kill. It was as she was absorbed in her task that she heard someone say her name.

"Keira?"

She looked over, expecting it to be Anita, and was surprised to see someone different, though vaguely familiar.

"You don't remember me, do you?" the woman said. "I spoke to you in the dining room a few days ago. About your article. I'm here with a bachelorette party."

It clicked into place in Keira's mind. The blond Texan woman with the heart-shaped face who'd produced a picture of Keira and Cristiano.

"Oh yes, of course," she said. "How's it going?"

The woman seemed shy, a little awkward, Keira thought. Then she remembered how she'd practically bitten her head off for approaching her last time and understood why there was an air of trepidation about her.

"I wanted to apologize," the woman told her. "For interrupting you that night. You must get it all the time."

Keira shook her head. "Not at all. I'm sorry for being frosty. Let's start again." She held her hand out to shake the woman's. "I'm Keira, and it's really nice to meet someone who's read my work."

The woman blushed and shook her extended hand. "You could call me a fan," she said with a shrug.

"Do you have a name?" Keira joked.

"Oh, haha. Yes. I'm Steph." Her blush deepened. "My friends are over there." She pointed at the rest of the wedding party, who were watching the exchange with rapt attention. "They're all fans too."

"I'm not going to lie," Keira said. "But this feels really strange!"

"Are you on a date?" Steph asked, eyeing the spare wine glass. "I can go."

Keira shook her head. "Nope. No date. I'm just waiting for Juliet. She's one of my interviewees for this season's article."

Steph's eyes widened. "That's so cool. I'd love to be in one of your articles."

Keira gestured to her spare seat. "Well then, why not?" she said. "I've got some time to kill, and I'm sure you have some interesting insights into love and romance to give me."

She remembered how Nina had specifically asked her to interview locals but they seemed in short supply on a tourist ship. Other than possibly the captain and the crew, she probably wasn't going to meet a "local" until they arrived in Finland the next morning.

Steph looked bowled over with enthusiasm at the prospect of being in Keira's hot seat. "Emma might be a better person to speak to. She's the bride-to-be, after all."

Keira looked over at where Steph was indicating, to a woman amongst the rest of the group. Just then, she saw Anita heading her way.

"Here's an idea," Keira said to Steph. "Why don't I come and sit with you a little later this evening? I'm a bit busy right now, but I'm planning on going to the live music and dance later. We could all meet up there, and make a night of it."

"Really?" Steph said, her eyes bulging. "You want to hang out with us?"

Keira couldn't help but find it strange that she could have such an effect on someone. "I assure you, I'm a completely normal person." She smiled. "How about after dinner? Eight?"

"That's amazing!" Steph exclaimed. She squealed and hurried away to tell the group her news.

Anita pulled up alongside Keira. "What was that about?" she asked.

"Oh, I'm sure you get it all the time," Keira said, flicking her hair jokingly. "Just a fan."

Anita laughed.

CHAPTER THIRTEEN

The moment Keira set foot in the dance hall, she was glad she'd made the effort to come. It was insane, a huge, windowless room, with large, sweeping gold staircases leading down to a central, oval-shaped floor. There was a stage at one end, with a faux stained glass window behind it, chandeliers of dripping glass hanging from the center of the domed ceiling, and bright disco lights that turned the whole space from purple, to blue, to red.

Keira stood at the top of the steps, gazing down with surprise. It wasn't particularly to her taste, and was verging on tacky, but it was definitely something unique for her, and she was eager to enjoy her evening. Especially since the band was a proper five-piece jazz band, with a double bassist, drummer, pianist, guitarist, and saxophonist. Noise pulsed up the steps at her, as well as heat coming from the jiving bodies below.

"Keira?" a voice said.

She turned and saw Anita. They'd shared a glass of wine together before parting ways to eat and dress for the evening. She looked stunning in a floor-length red silk dress and matching colored flower in her dark hair, which she'd pinned back. Keira had worn the one nice dress she'd brought with her, black, thigh-length, with a deep plunging V neck that bordered on risky. It was the one item of clothing that always made her feel sexy, but she felt very plain in comparison to Anita.

"You look awesome," Keira said, kissing Anita on the cheek.

"I'm on a mission," Anita told her, wiggling her eyebrows.

"You are?" Keira asked, curiously.

"Yup. I'm looking for a man tonight. A fling. It's well overdue." She checked her watch, as if it were somehow keeping track of her sexual conquests.

Keira laughed. Anita reminded her a bit of Bryn, if her sister's craziness was replaced by calm, emotionless determination.

"Well, I don't think you'll have any trouble looking like that," Keira told her.

Anita smirked. "What about you?"

"Am I looking for a fling?" Keira asked, raising her eyebrows. "No way. I'm strictly celibate at the moment. It's part of the

71

assignment *not* to fall in love. At least for two weeks." She chuckled.

"That's stupid," Anita said, plainly.

"I'm on a sort of voyage of self-discovery," Keira told her, her tongue only slightly in her cheek, making note of the boating metaphor she'd accidentally uttered. "I'm trying not to rebound."

"But why?" Anita asked, looking confused. "Rebounds are the whole point of ending relationships. Aren't they?"

"Don't say that," Keira chuckled in response. "I don't exactly have a choice. It's part of the job. And I can go without a man for two weeks." On second thought, she added, "I hope."

"Are you really telling me you never lie?" Anita asked. "No one at your magazine will know if you have a one-night stand if you don't tell them."

She was right, Keira admitted to herself, but she wasn't good at lying. Besides, she wanted to challenge herself. It wasn't just Nina and Elliot who were steering her behavior, but herself, her own desire not to damage her heart any further.

They heard noise coming from behind them then and both turned to see the bachelorette party arrive. Keira saw Steph among the group and waved. Steph directed the other women over.

"Hi." Keira smiled. "You guys look great. I can't wait to pick all your brains."

Steph looked thrilled. "This is Emma," she said, introducing the bride-to-be. "And that's Kate, Johanna, Nala and Unice." She pointed to each woman as she said their names, and Keira made a mental note to remember while quite confident that she wouldn't.

"Shall we head down to the dance floor?" Keira asked the group.

"The bar first," Anita interrupted. "I need a cocktail. Or two."

Everyone laughed, and they went down the sweeping gold staircase, descending into the warmth, noise, and bright lights of the dance hall. The bar was crowded.

"I've got this, ladies," Anita said. "Mojitos all round?"

The girls of the bachelorette party nodded with excitement and watched as the lithe Anita wove through the crowds, declaring herself to be "Juliet" as she went. Most people must have recognized her from the afternoon matinee performances because they all moved aside.

"Have you ever used your fame to get to the front of a line?" Steph asked Keira.

"I'm not famous," Keira replied. "And even if I was, I'd *never* do that! I don't have the guts."

"You should," Emma piped up. She had the same accent as Steph, like a southern belle. "It's like having a superpower and choosing not to use it."

Keira laughed, but she couldn't share their sentiments. She was nowhere near well known enough to pull the "don't you know who I am?" card, and besides, she *hated* those self-entitled types. Becoming one was definitely not on her list of things to do.

It didn't take long for Anita to get to the front of the bar, and once there she was recognized by the barman, who ignored all the others who'd been waiting and went straight to her. They watched him lean forward and her speak in his ear, then he shook his head as if rejecting her order, turned to the fridge behind him, and pulled out an oversized bottle of champagne. Keira's eyes widened.

"That's not for us, is it?" she exclaimed.

Emma started clapping. "I can already tell this is going to be the best night of my life!"

Keira was a little reticent, however. She didn't want to get too drunk again, like she had the night she'd thrown the drink at Rob. Besides, she was working and she had to remain professional.

Anita made it back with the huge bottle in one hand and flutes in the other. She cheered loudly.

"Did you get that for free?" Keira asked, her eyes wide.

Anita nodded. "Yeah, that's Danny. I've worked on a ship with him before. We have a thing going." She winked, then handed a glass to each of the women and, without missing a beat, popped the cork of the champagne bottle. Everyone cheered.

Keira watched her own flute fill up with the enticing bubbly liquid. Free alcohol would be even harder to resist!

They found themselves a table at the edge of the dance floor, and then some of the girls headed off, Anita amongst them, to dance to the live jazz music. Keira stayed behind with Emma and her trusty notebook.

"I won't keep you for too long," Keira told her. "I know you'll want to be dancing."

"Are you kidding me?" Emma said. "I'm going to be in a Romance Guru article. This is the best bachelorette party ever!"

Keira smiled, touched that her articles could mean so much to someone. "Why don't you start by telling me about your fiancé?" she asked.

Emma smiled and sunk her chin onto her fist. "Nate. Oh, he's just wonderful."

"How did you meet?"

"Through a friend. I'd tried all the dating apps, but at the end of the day it just works better when there's some kind of actual link there, you know? It's like they've already gone through one vetting process." She laughed.

Keira wrote down her words. "That makes sense," she admitted. "So how long did it take before you knew you wanted to marry him?"

"It was pretty much instant," Emma said. "Love at first sight." She sighed dreamily.

Keira had long ago given up believing in love at first sight, but she wrote down Emma's words nonetheless. Who was she to challenge her opinion anyway? Just because she'd been jaded by heartache didn't mean everyone had.

"Was the feeling mutual?" Keira asked.

Emma barked out a laugh then. "Absolutely not. He thought I was irritating. It was hard work convincing him I was worthy of his time."

"Oh? And how did you achieve that?"

"I just hung around like a bad smell," Emma said, chuckling. "I figured if I was just there I'd become familiar. It also meant I could block other women from getting at him. He's very attractive so I have to beat them off sometimes."

Keira recalled the stress that had come with being Cristiano's partner. He was so good-looking that women fell over themselves swooning over him, and it meant Keira had been in a perpetual state of insecurity. Every woman was a potential competitor. It had been a suffocating mind-set to inhabit.

"Is he on his bachelor party as well?" Keira asked.

Emma nodded. "Yes. And I know what you're thinking. Who's keeping an eye on him? Well, I have a best male friend who's gone along as my spy. We made a pact that he would tell me everything that happened. I can't go into marriage without complete trust."

Keira thought that there was a bit of contradiction there. She was spying on her partner in order to trust him? Didn't make too much sense to her.

"Well, Emma, thanks for your insight," Keira said. "Shall we go dance now?"

Emma nodded, and they headed off to join the others on the dance floor. The music was awesome, and thanks to the small glass of champagne Keira had been sipping slowly, the bubbles had made her feel looser and freer. It felt great to let her hair down, and not with a guy but with a group of fun-loving women.

No sooner had she thought the words than a guy wove through the crowd toward the group. He made a beeline straight for Keira, touching her bare arm lightly.

"You're the prettiest girl in here," he said.

Keira raised an eyebrow. "That's a very bold starting line."

"I don't like to waste time," he replied.

"Me neither," Keira replied. "So I may as well tell you now I'm not interested. I'm here with some girlfriends. I'm not looking for a man."

"Fair enough," he replied, letting go of her arm. He turned to the side to where Anita was dancing beside her. Keira watched on, stunned, as he touched her arm and said the exact same thing to her. Only this time it worked, and Anita giggled before allowing herself to be pulled into a dance with the man.

When Keira turned back to the main group, she noticed that all the girls were looking about them with confusion. She realized Emma wasn't there.

"Did she go to the bar?" Keira asked.

Steph shook her head. "No. She got a phone call and then just ran away."

Keira immediately thought of the male friend she'd sent to spy on her fiancé. Had the call she'd been dreading come in?

"We should find her," Nala added.

"What about Anita?" Steph asked.

"I think she's fine," Unice said, laughing, casting her eyes over at Anita in the embrace of the man, swaying together to the music.

Just then, Keira noticed a figure on the gold staircase, hurrying up with a phone in one hand. It was Emma.

"There she is!" Keira called out.

The rest of the group headed away, weaving through the crowds toward the gold stairs, pushing past pulsing bodies. They made it to the bottom of the staircase and hurried up. Emma had disappeared from sight.

They reached the top, panting, and headed out the huge doors. Emma was in the corridor, slumped in a heap, weeping. Her cell phone lay discarded beside her.

"What happened?" Steph cried, racing to her friend.

"Nate called off the wedding!" Emma cried.

Everyone looked stunned. Keira gasped.

"That was him on the phone?" Kate asked. She didn't seem completely convinced that the wedding was off. "You heard it from his mouth? It wasn't one of the others pulling a sick prank?"

Emma shook her head emphatically. She spoke through her sobs, each one of her words spoken like an angry punch. "I know Nate's voice. He said it didn't feel right. He said he was losing himself in the relationship!" she wailed, and sunk her face into her arms.

Keira felt terrible for her. And also like a voyeur imposing on a private moment. This wasn't her tragedy to witness. She took a step back at the same time the rest of the party rushed in. They formed something of a protective barrier around Emma as she wailed.

"I gave up so much for him! And he says *he's* lost in the relationship?"

Her cries were half anger, half agony. Keira could almost feel Emma's heart breaking.

She felt too awkward to stay around any longer. The women were in a huddle, Keira completely forgotten in their focus on their devastated friend. She turned and walked away, feeling shell-shocked by how her evening had ended.

Keira headed back to her room. Suddenly she felt unable to use any of the interview with Emma that she'd conducted. It wouldn't be right to publish words she'd said about what she felt was a loving relationship. Keira knew all too well the pain it would cause her, because she felt that agony every time she saw the magazine cover of her and Cristiano, or every time someone asked her how he was.

She went to her desk and sat down, unsure what to do, what to use of her evening. Nina's brief had been very clear: interact with people. But if she couldn't use any specifics, what was she to do? She could change the names but it would still be obvious to Emma when she read the article, and Keira felt more loyalty to a fan and reader than she did to her bosses who seemed to be using her at the moment.

She decided instead to write a philosophical passage, which was completely the opposite of what Nina had requested.

How blissful love can be, she wrote, *but how it can be blinding and painful, too. After a particularly wonderful evening in the dance hall of the cruise ship, dancing to exceptional live jazz music in the company of some of the most fun, powerful women I've ever been honored to meet, I'm left wondering how much of oneself must be sacrificed in order to build a shared life with someone else. And what is the difference between sacrifice and compromise? Must we sacrifice parts of ourselves in order to be with someone?*

CHAPTER FOURTEEN

Keira was mid-breakfast when she heard the announcement come over the PA that the ship was pulling into Helsinki. She was relieved to know she'd soon be on solid ground, and also glad to know she'd have more opportunities to speak to locals about Scandinavian-style love. Her interviews on the cruise ship had been pretty disastrous. As she'd sat up last night trying to work out what to write for Nina and Elliot, it had been nearly impossible. Salvaging something from the wreckage of Emma's interview was like drawing blood from a stone, and she already knew *Viatorum* wouldn't be impressed with what she'd done.

She took the final sip of coffee just as a group of women entered the dining room. It was the bachelorette party from last night, all looking worse for wear. Emma's eyes were puffy and red. Unice was cradling an arm around her, leading her like a zombie toward a table. Keira hesitated, wondering whether she should go over and speak to them. But it just felt too intrusive. What was the use in being friendly when yesterday she'd silently excused herself from the unfolding drama, evaporating into the ether without a word?

Keira decided Emma and her friends probably wouldn't want her to speak to them, so she packed her notebook and pen in her purse, then stood and headed for the door. But her attempt at a swift exit was noticed.

"Keira, hey!"

She looked up and saw Steph waving at her. She looked as terrible as Emma, Keira thought, with dark purple bags under her eyes. Keira wondered whether any of the women had gotten any sleep last night at all. She stepped toward them cautiously.

"What happened to you last night?" Steph continued. "You disappeared. I was wondering if maybe you'd ended up finding a sexy guy like Anita had."

Keira smiled awkwardly. "No. I just headed to my room to get some work done. Looming deadline and all that."

Steph must have noticed her hesitation because an expression of awkwardness overcame her features, as though she was considering whether calling Keira over had been misjudged. But it wasn't her, Keira reasoned in her mind, it was the situation. It just felt so intrusive being here, witnessing Emma's pain, being involved in any way during this tragic time. It wasn't her place.

"I'd better go," Keira said, gripping the strap of her purse tightly. "We only have a day in Helsinki. I want to make the most of it."

Steph nodded, looking lackluster. "Yeah. Sure. Bye." Her tone had become blank.

Keira hurried away, feeling awful. She wondered what Steph thought of her, if she considered her to be a bit of a prima donna, or too big for her boots. She wondered whether she'd disappointed a *fan*.

Getting off the boat was an exceptional relief. Even though the wind was colder than any she'd ever felt, it was so refreshing to be off the ship, out of the stagnant air and breathing what seemed to be pure oxygen. The tip of her nose smarted within minutes, but she felt rejuvenated.

The first word that sprang to her mind as she walked the streets of Helsinki was *cute,* which Keira knew all too well had no place in a romance article. But from the trams to the Victorian-era lamp posts, to the abundance of trees decorated with sparkling silver lights, Helsinki looked like a film set for the most cozy Christmas movie ever. On top of it all, the locals seemed to have a very quirky sense of fashion that just added to the quaintness.

Around every street corner, Keira found cute glass-fronted stores selling things like vintage crockery and clothes, old vinyl records, and knitted winter wear. The urge to spend all her money here was enormous!

Keira wandered along the patterned brick-paved streets, watching the passing cyclists and trams. Then up ahead, Keira caught sight of a cute little tea room, decorated with chintzy floral bunting. She was in need of warming up, and felt drawn to the sweet-looking store. She decided it would be a good spot to get some interviews, and so she went inside.

The cafe was much smaller than Keira had anticipated. In fact, there were only about six tables, with two chairs each, and currently none of them were occupied. She must be too early for the tea shift.

She was about to turn around and leave when the woman behind the counter—a lady with a mass of blond curls like a lion's mane—grinned at her widely.

"*Hei!*"

"Oh, hello," Keira said, feeling shy. "Sorry to disturb you. I'm not stopping."

"But why not?" the woman asked, immediately switching to English.

Keira took a breath. "I'm a writer. I was looking for people to interview about romance in Helsinki. I thought there'd be people inside but since there aren't I ought to leave."

"You can interview me," the woman replied. She had an incredibly cheerful expression, with dimples either side of her mouth. Her demeanor was inviting. "And I can serve you some remarkable tea while you do."

"Remarkable?" Keira quipped. "How can I resist?"

She took a seat at a rickety wooden table painted powder blue.

From behind the counter, the woman called out, "What do you like? White, black, or green?" A soft clinking sound echoed around the small empty room as she took a delicate tea cup and saucer down from a little shelf beside her head.

"I have no idea," Keira confessed. "I'm a coffee drinker."

"Of course." The woman smiled. "You're American. In that case, I will give you the best introduction to tea. Everyone loves it. Coco vanilla rooibos."

"Sounds great," Keira said. It was all the same to her, since she had no clue either way.

She took her notebook out of her purse.

"So," she began, looking up at the woman as she bustled around preparing a pot of tea. "Why don't you tell me your name to start?"

"Venla," the woman said.

Keira jotted it down. It was unfamiliar to her, but very pretty. "And this is your business?"

"It is. It's my baby."

Keira thought of Elliot's relationship with *Viatorum*, which she usually thought of as more his husband than his child. A child was someone you nurtured and cared for, whereas a husband was someone to nag and make demands of.

"How long have you been running it?" Keira asked, genuinely interested.

"Years," the woman told her, in her jolly voice. She began pouring boiling water into the teapot. "People in Helsinki just can't get enough tea."

She finished what she was doing, placing the pot, mug, and saucer on a battered-looking tray, then carried it over to the rickety table.

"Let that brew for at least three minutes," she said, taking the seat opposite Keira.

"Thanks," Keira replied. "I can't wait." She hadn't realized how cold her fingers had become. Finland was even colder than Denmark had been. "I'm surprised it hasn't snowed," she commented.

"It will," Venla replied.

"Today?" Keira asked, raising her eyebrows. The thought appealed to her. Although she wasn't sure what the deal would be aboard the ship. Could ships get snowed in? "Anyway," she said, bringing her attention back to the interview. "Do you mind answering a few questions for me? About love and dating in Finland?"

"I can try," Venla laughed. "Although I don't have that much experience."

"No?" Keira asked, quizzically. "Maybe you should start there."

"Well, I've been with my partner longer than I've owned my shop," she said, smiling. "I've never really dated. We just found one another and that was that."

"That sounds... wonderful," Keira mused. Imagine never dating. It was like a dream come true! "How did you meet?"

"I can't quite remember. The cinema, I think. Yes, that's right. She was buying popcorn."

Keira raised her eyebrows. "You just started speaking?"

Venla nodded, like it was the most natural thing in the world. "Yes. I said *hei*. She said *hei*. We talked. Now here we are twenty years later."

Keira was stunned. If only things could be that simple at home. "There weren't any mind games? No chasing?"

"No, no, no, I don't like that sort of stuff. I don't think many Finns do. And we don't have any of those silly rules about who makes the first moves, or how many days to leave before you call, or how many dates until you can sleep together."

"It all sounds very..." Keira struggled for the word. What she was really thinking was *bland*. The rules, the "silly" games, were almost half of the fun. Finally, she settled on "...Pragmatic."

"I suppose you could say that," Venla agreed. "But it saves a lot of time. Then we have more time for snuggling and taking saunas."

"Well, okay, *that* does sound good." Keira chuckled.

Venla poured Keira's tea and watched her eagerly. "It's ready now. I hope you like it."

Keira picked it up and took a sip. It was pretty good, not to mention very warming. She felt the feeling return to her fingertips. "Mm, yes, that's lovely."

She sipped the tea and returned her notebook to her purse.

"Is the interview over?" Venla asked. She chuckled. "That was painless."

"It was an interview, not an interrogation," Keira quipped.

"So what is your plan for the day?"

"I'm going on a walking tour after lunch. Although I kind of wish I was going to a sauna now that you've mentioned it."

"To find a lover?"

Keira choked on her sip of tea. She coughed. "Oh. No. That's not my intention."

"No? You don't want to find yourself a Finn to keep you warm?"

Keira blushed. "I'm only here for a day. I don't think it would be sensible. Besides, my assignment during this trip is to not rebound."

Venla looked confused. "Are you a freelancer? Or do your employers demand this? Your boss surely cannot dictate your life that way."

"Oh, it's not like that," Keira said, feeling awkward. "It's a mutual agreement."

But as soon as she said it, she realized how far from the truth that statement now was. Maybe once it had been a mutual agreement, but somewhere along the line things had transformed. She had not given the go-ahead for this trip, had not given the green light for another assignment, and Elliot had gone ahead and booked it anyway. It was just a fluke that they didn't ask her to attempt another romance this time. It wasn't because of her, or her heart, or her mental health that they'd made the decision, but because they'd done some market research, analyzed some data, and come to the conclusion that her readers wanted to see her alone, for one trip at least. The thought settled in Keira's stomach, making her feel a little nauseous.

She finished her tea and stood. "I'd better get going. Thanks so much for speaking to me. You've been very helpful."

"When do I get to read your article?" Venla asked.

"It will be published by Christmas," Keira explained. She took a business card from her purse. She didn't usually hand them out, but Venla seemed keen. "I don't know if it will be your kind of thing, though," she explained, looking at the no-nonsense businesswoman. "It's all a bit... gooey."

"I may be a practical Finn but I love love as much as the next person," she said, taking the card and tucking it under the saucer on the table. "I look forward to reading it. Good luck."

Keira left Venla's tea room feeling like something had clicked in her mind. A new understanding had come over her. During the course of the conversation, she'd changed. In what way, she couldn't be certain, but it was unmistakable. And if just one hour in Helsinki could transform her, what could a whole day do?

CHAPTER FIFTEEN

Keira's walking tour was meeting at Kaisaniemi Park. She strode along the streets until the tip of a huge greenhouse loomed up ahead of her. As she got closer, she noticed a group of people had already begun to congregate by the entrance way to the park, next to a statue. She made a beeline for the one person who didn't have a camera slung around his neck, who she assumed to be the guide.

"Hi, I'm Keira, the writer from *Viatorum* magazine," she told him. She checked Heather's itinerary. "And you're Jossi?"

"Yes, that's correct," he replied.

He was an older man than she was expecting, with a face weathered by time, and ice-white, thinning hair. Keira couldn't be sure but she thought that he had an air of disdain about him, like he had taken an instant disliking to her. She wondered if she was just being paranoid.

"So, you're supposed to be asking my clients questions about love, are you?" he asked.

Keira blushed. It sounded dumb when he put it like that. "Actually, I'm not planning on interviewing anyone during the tour," she explained. "I want to learn about Helsinki. This is for the *travel* part of the article."

He raised an eyebrow. "There's a travel part, is there? I thought it was all fluff."

Keira grimaced. She couldn't help but be a little offended by his tone. It wasn't like he had a particularly worthwhile job either, showing people around landmarks!

She hung back, watching as more people approached and joined the group. When there were about twenty or so people, Jossi checked his watch, then looked up.

"Right," he said in a loud voice. "Let's get this started."

Keira thought he sounded irritated to be there. Her initial offense gave way to curiosity.

Jossi began the tour, pointing at the statue beside them. "This is *Convolvulus*, a statue by Viktor Jansson."

He began to walk through the park, leading the group out onto the streets to a large square.

83

"Sennate Square," he announced. "Here we can see numerous examples of Carl Ludvig Engel's architecture. Over here we have the statue of Emperor Alexander, erected in 1894. It was built to commemorate the initiation of several reforms that increased Finland's autonomy from Russia."

Keira frowned. "I didn't even realize Finland used to be part of Russia."

Jossi nodded. "Yes. Now our country is officially called the Republic of Finland, but back in 1809 we were part of the Russian Empire, right up until the revolution in 1917 when we declared independence."

Keira was fascinated. "That's amazing. I had no idea."

For the first time, Jossi's defenses seemed to come down a little. He regarded her as if seeing for the first time someone who was eager to learn, who wanted to be educated, rather than some silly romantic American.

"Are you really interested in Finnish history?" he asked. "Most people just want to take photos of statues. No one ever listens to what I have to say."

"I'm interested," Keira said, nodding.

Jossi looked impressed.

They headed on to the next location, and as they walked, Jossi told Keira more about the history of the place. As he'd predicted, the rest of the group didn't seem interested at all. They just wanted photographs. But Keira listened with rapt attention as he told her how Finland was the first country in the world to grant all adults the right to vote, and about the Soviet Union attempting to occupy Finland during World War II but being ultimately unsuccessful. She absorbed all the information like a sponge.

Jossi led them through the Kauppatori Market, past the *Havis Amanda*, a nude female statue, and on to the restaurant-filled streets of Esplanadi.

As they walked and chatted, Jossi seemed to warm considerably, becoming quite animated, leaving his frosty persona behind him. In fact, he reminded Keira somewhat of Felix, with a calm, grandfatherly aura.

They reached their final stop on the tour, the Temppeliaukio Church. Jossi's guiding duties were over, and the group dispersed throughout the church, leaving just him and Keira behind.

"It's over?" she asked, feeling a little disappointed. She'd adored the tour, seeing so much of the city, and Jossi imparting his wisdom on her.

"Yes. But so is my shift," Jossi said. "If you want, I can show you around some more."

Keira had a sudden flash of an image, of her and Jossi, like Felix and Bryn, going for ten-kilometer runs before breakfast, shopping for furniture. But of course, that wasn't her. She wasn't even attracted to Jossi. He certainly wasn't attracted to her. It was just an innocent offer.

She let the silly imagery fade from her mind and looked up at Jossi, smiling.

"I'd like that," she agreed.

*

Jossi took her to the Helsinki Cathedral, a centrally located and formidable-looking building of white stone and turquoise domed turrets. His specialty was churches. Keira couldn't help but draw parallels in her mind with Cristiano, who adored church architecture.

The cathedral grounds were filled with tourists, but Jossi knew exactly where to go to get away from the crowds, showing Keira some shops and cafes tucked away from the main paths.

"Have you always lived in Helsinki?" Keira asked Jossi as they turned down a quiet alleyway.

"Oh no," he chuckled. "I spent months of my life in Nepal."

"Nepal?" Keira asked, surprised.

He laughed, as though delighted by her reaction. "Yes. In my youth, I was a mountaineer."

Keira's eyes widened further. "Nepal. That's where Everest is, right?"

Crinkles of happiness appeared at the sides of Jossi's eyes. "You're correct."

"Did you…"

"Summit Everest? Almost. But my climbing partner got into difficulties during our summit attempt and we had to turn back. We were only a few feet from the top of the world."

"That must have been, I don't know…" Keira said, pondering. "…hard. Turning back, I mean."

"Perhaps it would have been hard, but my climbing partner was also my wife, so there wasn't that much of a moral dilemma involved."

"Your wife," Keira repeated aloud. She hadn't meant to, but she felt herself straying into interview territory. Suddenly, she wanted to know all about Jossi and his life climbing mountains with his wife. It was so far from her own life, and it fascinated her. "Can you tell me about her?"

"Of course," Jossi said. "We did everything together. Partners in all senses of the word. Equals. We climbed amazing peaks, all over the world. Everest was on our wish list but it just wasn't meant to be."

"The equality you mentioned," Keira said. "Do you think that was a mountaineering thing, or a Finnish thing?"

He chuckled. "Maybe a bit of both." Then he shook his head. "No. Actually. It is a Finnish thing. Definitely. And probably why we were such a successful pair on the mountains. When you share the washing up and laundry, it is not such a stretch to share responsibilities on a cliff face."

"You shared chores?"

"Oh yes. And this was back in the seventies." He laughed again. "I'd never expect my wife to wash my socks without reciprocating the favor."

"That sounds… well, pretty great," Keira admitted.

Jossi laughed again. "It's strange to me that a young woman in the free world would find that unusual."

They'd just reached a cafe, and Jossi gestured toward it. "Would you like a tea? To warm yourself up? We've been outside for hours now."

Keira suddenly became aware of her frozen extremities. "Yes, that would be a good idea."

They headed for the cafe door, and Keira realized that Jossi wasn't hurrying to open it for her. That equality he spoke of also meant no chivalry. She thought of Cristiano, forever pulling chairs for her, taking her jacket from her. She wasn't sure if a sacrifice of chivalry was worth it for someone to wash your socks every two weeks.

Inside the cafe, it was very warm and the windows were steamed up. They took a seat beside the window on a long bench that stretched the length of it. A server came over and they both ordered tea. Keira felt more comfortable doing so now since her education in Venla's teashop.

When the server returned with their drinks, she gave Keira a curious look.

"This is a strange question," she said. "But are you that model from *Viatorum*?"

Keira's eyes widened with surprise. "I'm a writer for them," she explained. "Not a model."

"But that is you on the cover, isn't it? On the Paris skyline?" She pointed, and Keira realized with mortification that there was a stack of glossy magazines on the table before them, and staring right up at her were her and Cristiano.

Keira hunkered down. "Yes," she said sheepishly.

"I knew it!" the server exclaimed. "I love that photo. It's so classy. Oh, and the article, of course. It was awesome. Are you writing more?"

Keira felt her cheeks turn red. "Yes. I'm writing a piece on Helsinki."

"Amazing!" the girl said. "Can I take a picture for my profile?"

Keira could feel Jossi staring at her with surprise. She felt incredibly awkward. "Uh, yeah," she said to the server. "I guess."

The girl pulled a cell phone out of her pocket and positioned herself beside Keira. She pressed her cheek against Keira's and took a selfie.

"Thanks so much," she gushed, before scurrying away.

Keira smiled shyly. After taking a moment to collect herself, she turned to look at Jossi. His expression was one of thorough amusement.

"So, you're a celebrity, are you?" he joked, picking up the magazine.

"No way," Keira refuted. "I'm just a writer. That's all. The cover was my boss's idea."

"Who is the man?" Jossi asked, glancing at Cristiano.

Keira felt her insides churn. She wanted to lie, to say he was just a model hired for the day, but found herself instead revealing the truth.

"My ex," she said.

Jossi raised an eyebrow. "What happened?"

Keira's face was still very hot, and she could feel sweat collecting on the back of her neck. "It didn't work out. The distance. The pressure of work and travel. It just wasn't right in the end."

"Mmm," Jossi said, flipping through the pages of the magazine. "It is strange how fate works that way sometimes."

"What do you mean?" Keira asked.

He seemed to have become quite mellow.

"Well, I mean, that you are only here for one day. And that perhaps if you'd been here longer I may have asked you out."

Keira felt the uncomfortable pit in her stomach open up. Not because Jossi was too old for her, but because she realized, with surprise, that she might have agreed to date him. His company was enthralling. The age difference didn't really matter when the chemistry was so strong. She understood, at last, what the deal was with Bryn and Felix. But Jossi was right. Fate was standing in the way.

"I would've said yes, for the record," she told him.

Jossi nodded, like it was understood. They fell back into silence, a future that would never come to fruition hanging between them.

*

Saying goodbye to Jossi was quick, and relatively painless. They both approached it like ripping off a Band-Aid. A quick hug, a tight handshake, and then they parted, neither looking over their shoulder.

Keira headed back to the ship, filled with melancholy, but also feeling like a different person than the one who'd arrived here this morning. The whistle-stop tour of Helsinki had had a profound effect on her. For the first time, she knew exactly what she wanted to write, exactly how to approach her article.

But when she boarded the ship, she didn't head straight to her room to write. She went up to the deck, her arms crossed tightly about her middle, and watched as the boat pulled away from the harbor. As the city of Helsinki disappeared from sight, snow began to fall.

CHAPTER SIXTEEN

The ship continued, journeying onward to Stockholm, Sweden. In her cozy cabin, Keira awoke and began getting herself ready for the day. She washed and chose a comfortable outfit fit for the freezing weather she was bracing herself for.

As she dried her hair in front of the mirror, Keira thought back over her time in Helsinki. Spending time with Jossi had been really nice, without the pressure of any real romantic attraction. It had been more of a meeting of minds, a connection of souls, rather than anything else, and she cherished the experience. And thanks to him, she'd produced the best work of her trip thus far. Maybe even her career.

She'd just finished making herself up for the day when her phone began to ring. She looked over at it sitting on the table beside her bed and saw *Viatorum*'s name flashing up. She groaned, not in the mood for another check-in from Nina, especially after having sent her such a great passage yesterday. The last thing she wanted was to get an earful over something she was so proud of.

"Yes, Nina?" she asked in a drone voice as she answered the call.

"No," came Elliot's voice. "It's me."

"Oh," Keira replied, a little shocked. It wasn't often Elliot called directly. It still made her heart hitch with anxiety to speak to him on the phone. "Is everything okay?"

"Yes. It's fine. I'm just calling to say that your last passage was great. You struck the perfect tone. Can you make sure you carry on like that when you're in Sweden?"

"Like what exactly?" Keira asked. She didn't want there to be any crossed wires, although she pretty much knew exactly what Elliot was about to say.

"More interactions with men," Elliot confirmed. "It's great to see you turn them down, to learn from them. It's much better as a reader to see you learn about those cultural differences through experience rather than second hand like you did with Romeo and Juliet."

Keira had expected precisely this kind of comment from Elliot. But even though she was anticipating it, it still infuriated her to hear it.

"I'm not going to put myself out there if I don't want to," she explained, trying to sound calm, trying to channel some of Venla's authority. "What happened with Jossi was a natural occurrence. I'm not going to cultivate it."

There was a pregnant pause.

"Why not?" Elliot asked, sounding as clueless as always.

"I don't want to hurt people," she explained, leaving off that the person getting hurt more often than not was herself. "I don't like it."

Elliot left another long silence. "I don't understand what the problem is, Keira. I'm guiding you, giving you feedback, and helping you become the best writer you can be. I don't know why you're pushing back against that."

Keira gritted her teeth. She hadn't been planning on having this conversation with Elliot today, here in her cabin. She'd wanted to speak to him once she was back in New York, on home turf, face to face. But there was no point skirting around the issue any longer.

"Putting my heart on the line, time and time again," she said, "is very tiring. Emotionally. I've explained this to you before. You agreed after Paris that you would let me make the decisions, that I'd be in control going forward. And now you're going against that."

Elliot sighed. "I'm sorry, okay? There are a million things going on in my head. You're not the only person I'm overseeing, you know?" Another sigh. "But look, I get it. Next trip, you can pick everything, okay? Even the topic. Hell, you can stop being the Romance Guru if you really want. We've got a ton of amazing up and comings on staff at the moment. Meredith would take it over in a heartbeat."

Keira bit her lip. Maybe she'd been pushing back too much, acting ungrateful. Or maybe Elliot was just threatening her. It was hard to tell. The important thing to take from the conversation, though, was that for this assignment at least, she was going to have to follow *Viatorum*'s rules. And that meant putting herself out there again, putting her heart on the line.

To Elliot, she replied, with an air of finality in her voice, "Fine. For this assignment. Then we'll talk about it."

Elliot didn't utter another word. The call cut out and Keira felt her heart sink.

*

During breakfast, the now-familiar PA announcement was made. The ship would be docking at Stockholm harbor in approximately thirty minutes. Keira tried to take the conversation with Elliot in her stride, but it was playing on her mind more than she'd care to admit. A strange sense of foreboding had settled in her chest.

It took a lot of concentration to force the feelings to the back of her mind. The ship was docking in Sweden for three whole days, and after that she would be staying in a hotel for a further eight days. Now was the chance to really enjoy herself. The stop-start, stop-start of the assignment thus far had wreaked havoc with her routine, and the demands from Nina to include references to the cruise ship felt disingenuous. Everything was impacting on her writing. And that wasn't even to mention the rocking motion of the boat, which made the physical act of writing more difficult. Having ten full days in one place would give her the time she needed to relax and settle, to get her head around the piece as a whole, and to hopefully add some more words that would satisfy Nina and Elliot's demands without ruining her own emotional health in the process.

Keira looked through Heather's itinerary. There was an hour-long guided tour of the Royal Palace, Kungliga Slottet, starting mid-morning, but the rest of the day was hers to do with as she wished. She looked through the guide that had been provided by the ship, jotting down some locations in her notebook that she wanted to see during the next ten days, including museums, architectural sights of interest, and, of course, a ton of restaurants. Thanks to the ship food and her so-called diet, Keira hadn't sampled much in the way of Nordic cuisine. It didn't seem right not to write about food, particularly when eating had been such a central feature in her last few articles.

She finished the last sips of her coffee and went up on deck to watch the boat dock at the harbor. She loved this view, this first experience of a new city and new country, from the deck of a ship, from the ocean. It was magical and thrilling, and far more exciting than just arriving at an airport. She felt like she got a much better feel for a place when approaching it from the ocean, and it certainly made the unique flavors of the city more obvious. The architecture of Sweden, for example, looked very different from Denmark and Finland. It was grander, more imposing, and there were fewer quaint, colorful brick buildings. It was a city that meant business.

Keira smiled to herself as it came into sharper focus. The air was incredibly cold, making her skin tingle, and, feeling very underdressed, she quickly headed down to her room to wrap up in some extra layers.

By the time she was done layering up, the boat had finished docking, and she hurried off to begin her adventure in Stockholm.

Once on solid ground, she checked her map to plot out a route to the palace, and realized that it was far too far away to walk. She'd have to take a taxi. It was a bit of an oversight on Heather's part to arrange something so far from the harbor, and Keira was a little sad to have her favorite part of arriving in any city—the long, languid, aimless stroll through its streets—taken from her. Still, she hailed a cab and hopped in the back.

It was one of those rare occasions when Keira's driver was not bilingual. He frowned at her when she attempted to ask for the Kungliga Slottet, and she had to show him on the map what she meant. Then he gave her just one sharp nod and set off quickly.

Keira settled into her seat, a little concerned that she may have trouble talking to the locals here if speaking English wasn't as common as it was elsewhere in Europe. Language barriers had not been a problem for her so far, except for the elderly inn owner she'd met in Italy. Still, that had worked out pretty well so she wasn't too worried. She could handle a bit of awkward communication, and she still had her trusty translation app from her last trip!

The silent cab ride took just over half an hour, and Keira used the opportunity to gaze out the windows at the passing architecture. Sweden seemed very modern, more of a metropolis than her last two stops. A lot of the buildings were modern—vast, gray estates, surrounded by parking lots—that wouldn't have looked that out of place at home. There were no cobblestone sidewalks, no quaint tram lines, no cute vintage stores. Keira tried to reassure herself that her cab driver was taking her on the back routes to avoid traffic, but her foreboding feeling from earlier was starting to return. Of what she'd seen so far, Stockholm was the last of the three places she'd want to spend ten full days. She wished to be back in Finland.

But her mind was thoroughly changed when the cab pulled onto a gorgeous stone bridge, careened across a river, and pulled up outside the stunning royal palace. The architecture was breathtaking. Baroque, Keira noted, built from a combination of stone columns and pale orange brickwork, sleek and efficiently designed. All the buildings surrounding it—the parliamentary buildings, the national museum, and Skeppsholmen Church—had the same style of design, the same brick and stone combination. It gave the area an incredibly harmonious vibe. A few select trees were dotted around the otherwise paved, pedestrianized area.

Keira thanked her cab driver and hurried out, eager to see what the palace tour had in store for her.

In the courtyard, there was a row of impeccably dressed soldiers guarding the palace. Keira passed them, heading in through the main doors and stopping in the grand foyer. The space was vast, and a site map showed that there were lots of different things to see within the palace, including Royal Apartments, the Banquet Hall, King Carl Gustaf's Jubilee Room, the crown jewels in the Treasury, a collection of royal books in the Bernadotte Library, the Royal Armory, and several museums to explore. Keira couldn't wait to get started.

She turned on the spot, searching to see whether there was anyone who resembled a guide standing around, a white-haired Jossi type in a corduroy suit, or the tell-tale sign of a clump of tourists sporting long-lens cameras. But apart from Keira, the only person loitering in the reception area was a handsome young man who was far too young, she decided, to be a tour guide.

She went up to the reception desk, speaking to the suited man behind it.

"I'm supposed to be joining a tour," she explained. Looking at her watch, she added, "I may be a little early."

The man nodded. "Early, yes. But the guide is already here." He pointed, to Keira's surprise, at the handsome young man.

Keira raised her eyebrows. "He's the guide?"

The receptionist nodded. "MILO!" he called out to the young man.

The man's head turned, revealing to Keira piercing blue eyes. He had a warm face, with a large, inviting smile that revealed a set of straight, white teeth. Keira flushed with embarrassment as he came over to them.

"Sorry," she apologized immediately. "I didn't expect for you to be called over. If you're busy…"

"Not busy," Milo interrupted. He held his hand out for her to shake. "May I ask your name?"

"Keira," she replied, a little hesitant to make physical contact with someone so handsome.

"Keira Swanson?" he asked. "Are you the writer?"

"Yes," Keira replied, blushing. She felt suddenly very tongue-tied in Milo's presence, unsure of what to say. But his smile was so warm, his eyes so kind, and his demeanor so inviting, that she felt reassured. "I'm really excited to see the palace. How long have you been a guide here?"

Her question was twofold; though she did genuinely want to know, she also wanted to find out how old he might be. He looked to be very young to Keira, and it always unsettled her to be attracted to men younger than her. Cristiano had been, and that had ended terribly.

"Ever since I finished my master's," he explained. "So, gosh, I would guess now about eight years."

Keira did the math in her head quickly and concluded he was in his early thirties, and was alarmed when the first thought to cross her mind was *perfect.*

She wondered, with a sudden jolt of cynicism, whether this had been planned by her magazine. Perhaps Milo was a plant, a temptation, to see whether she could stick to her assignment. Then she checked herself. She was getting paranoid!

"What did you study?" Keira asked, intrigued. "For your master's, I mean?"

"History," Milo told her. He gestured to the palace and smiled. "Hence the job here."

"Yes, it's quite fitting, I suppose," Keira said with a blush, feeling suddenly dumb.

Tourists started filing into the palace, cameras in hand like weapons, and they crowded around Milo, jostling Keira out of the way. Keira noticed the adoring eyes of some of the women amongst the group, and she thought of Cristiano, of the way women swooned around him, and how uncomfortable it had made her feel to know she was just like them. It wasn't an experience she wanted to repeat anytime soon.

Once everyone had assembled, the tour began. Milo was extremely well informed, but considering he'd been doing this job for so long that was to be expected. Still, he divulged his knowledge with enthusiasm. Keira wondered whether he had to feign it a little after all these years, but she suspected Milo really was that into the palace and its history.

As they went, Keira took notes for her article later. She noticed that Milo kept looking over.

"Am I distracting you?" she asked.

"Not at all," he replied. "I'm just curious about your work."

Keira felt herself blush again and couldn't help but feel infuriated with herself. She was supposed to be on a voyage of self-discovery and independence, yet here she was getting weak at the knees at the first handsome man who'd shown a passing interest in her!

"It's not all that interesting," she said, snapping her notebook shut and slinging it into her purse. "In comparison to a palace filled with history anyway."

Milo smiled. "Yes, I love that feeling, of being surrounded by history. Knowing that the ground you're walking has been walked for hundreds of years by the nobility. I'm not one for ghosts or spirits, but there's no denying there's *something* in a place like this. It's like the walls remember."

Keira nodded. "I know exactly what you mean. I feel it too. I do every time I come to Europe, to be honest. Whenever I see all the old architecture, I can picture all the people through the ages who had seen it too. It's humbling, really."

"You've been elsewhere in Europe?" Milo asked.

"For my job," Keira explained. "I was in Paris last month. Italy before that. Ireland. Germany. Denmark. Finland." As she reeled off the locations she'd visited thanks to her job, she realized just what a charmed life she really lived. Though she had to keep in mind that it came with great sacrifices; relationships, apartments, her waistline!

"Wow, you've been to loads of places," Milo commented. "I'm not much of a traveler myself. I'm a... what's the correct term in English... homebody?"

Keira chuckled. "Yeah. That's right. I am too, to be honest. I miss New York a lot when I'm not there. Before this job, I barely even left the city!"

It felt so strange now to think about the person she used to be. It wasn't that long ago that she was in her apartment with Zach, trying desperately to get a writing job. Now look how far she'd come, how much her life had changed.

"See, to me," Milo said, "New York sounds very exciting. I'd love to visit one day. Although I don't know if I'd cope with the busy-ness."

"It's not that different from here," Keira told him. "Although way bigger. And there aren't any palaces, I'm afraid."

Milo chuckled then, and it suddenly struck Keira that they were sharing a very easy conversation. Maybe it was just Scandinavian men, she thought, who put her at ease in their company. Or maybe there was something special about Milo, as there had been with Jossi. In fact, she realized then that Milo reminded her of Jossi, of how she'd imagined he'd have been in his youth.

"Have you ever climbed a mountain?" Keira asked Milo, struck by a sudden curiosity.

Milo burst out laughing, clearly confused by her question. "Erm, no," he admitted. "Should I have?"

Keira laughed and shook her head. "No. Don't worry. Weird question."

They continued walking through the palace, Milo taking brief moments to impart his knowledge to the tourists before returning, each time, to Keira's side. And each time they engaged in warm conversation, making light jokes, revealing snippets of their lives and personalities. By the time the tour ended, Keira felt like she'd known Milo her whole life.

"What else is there to see in Stockholm?" she asked as the tourists dispersed, eager to remain in his company for as long as possible. It didn't matter that she'd already compiled a huge list of places she wanted to see in the city; any excuse to keep speaking to Milo.

He checked his watch. "I'm on my lunch break now," he said. "We could grab a coffee and I could recommend you some great places."

Keira was suddenly hesitant. Was Milo proposing a loose date? He was so attractive, so sweet and warm, that even a short coffee date would be dangerous. Her chances of falling for him were already too great, and she wanted to prove to herself—and her readers—that she didn't need a man. But at the same time, she could get some great material for her article. Elliot had asked for exactly this scenario. Perhaps if she approached the coffee date through the lens of a writer on an assignment, she'd be able to keep her raging hormones at bay.

"That would be great," she told him. "Will you let me interview you?"

"For your love article?" Milo replied. He looked a little shy for the first time, and shrugged. "I guess."

Keira pondered his response as they strolled out the palace doors and into the courtyard.

Milo directed her through the space and down an alleyway, where a small truck was selling coffee. She frowned in confusion as he went up and ordered takeout coffee. She'd been expecting a sit-down chat, but Milo clearly had no intentions of getting off his feet anytime soon.

"Where are we heading?" Keira asked, as he handed her a coffee.

"I wanted to show you the City Hall," he said. "It's one of Sweden's most famous buildings. Full of artwork. I got the impression you're a fan of galleries."

Keira was surprised, and touched, that he'd picked up on that from just the hour-long tour of the palace. He'd been paying attention to her. The thought made her stomach flutter.

Their route took them across one of the many bridges that spanned the river.

"It's so gorgeous here," Keira commented.

"Just wait until it snows," Milo said. "It's stunning then. And the sunsets are extraordinary."

"I'd love to see that," Keira replied. "Luckily I've got ten days in Stockholm so I've got plenty of time to."

"Ten days?" Milo asked, his eyebrows rising. "Most people who come on the cruise only stay for three."

"Yeah, but I'm not heading back with the ship," she explained. "I'm staying on in a hotel for an extra week and then flying home from Stockholm."

Keira tried to decipher Milo's expression. He looked glad, excited even. She wondered why. Was he thinking about seeing her again?

They made it to the City Hall and Keira was, as always, blown away by the architecture. It was a huge, red brick building, complete with columns and numerous windows. The whole ground floor was open air, a series of archways she could look straight through to the courtyard beyond. And the crowning glory was a huge brick observation tower stretching several floors into the air.

"This is amazing," Keira murmured absent-mindedly.

"I thought you'd like it," Milo commented. Then he added, "This is where they host the banquets for the Nobel peace prize."

"Cool," Keira replied.

"The tower," he said, pointing to the viewing tower she'd noticed before, "is one hundred and six meters high. Three hundred and sixty-five steps up. Want to go?"

Keira laughed. She was impressed by Milo's knowledge. But she was also feeling a little weary after the long tour and all the walking. Milo, on the other hand, seemed to have boundless energy.

"Actually, I wonder if we could sit somewhere?" Keira suggested. "My feet are a little sore and I don't think I'd manage three hundred and sixty-five steps."

"Of course," he said. Then from the corner of his mouth, he added, "I didn't really want to go up. I was just showing off. Now, my favorite cafe is just around the corner."

They headed away from the City Hall and Milo showed Keira into a quaint teashop that would have fit in nicely in Finland. It was nice to know that there was *some* cuteness in the city.

The woman behind the counter waved at Milo and spoke to him in Swedish. Clearly, he was a regular here. They took a seat in the window, which was always Keira's preferred place to sit because then she was able to people-watch. They didn't even need to order; two coffees were placed on the table before them by a server almost immediately.

"*Tack*," Milo said to the server.

Keira thought she noticed the woman wink as she walked away. She looked at Milo.

"*Tack*? Is that Swedish for thank you?"

He nodded. Keira held back from blurting out that it was the cutest word she'd heard so far.

"So," Milo said, taking a sip of coffee. "What do you want to put in your love article?"

Keira giggled. "Love article is a strange description. It really is just like a normal travel article, but approached from the perspective of a single woman trying to learn about different cultural approaches to love."

"And what have you learned so far? About Scandinavian men?" Milo asked. "Other than the fact we all have a little bit of Viking in our blood."

"I've learned you're not afraid of housework," she told him. "That women don't expect you to make the first move or hold doors open for them. And that you're unlikely to propose."

Milo nodded, looking impressed. "That's quite an accurate portrayal. And I wonder how you feel about that? Your last trip was to Italy, didn't you say? We must be quite different from Italian men. Isn't it all about chivalry and macho displays of aggression over there?"

He laughed, and held up his arm to mockingly show off his muscles, actually showing off his muscles in the process. Keira swallowed the lump in her throat.

"Yeah, that's right," she told him, as the memory of Cristiano's fist colliding with Zach's nose resurfaced in her mind's eye.

"It sounds like you've already done your research," Milo commented. "What else can you learn from me?"

Keira thought of Elliot's request, for her to learn through experience. She sipped her coffee quickly, feeling embarrassment creeping into her cheeks. "Uh, nothing specific. I just like to interview people so the articles aren't all about me, you know?"

"Well, I don't know what I'd be able to tell you, to be honest. I try not to dwell on the past. Each relationship is unique. It's two people bringing their different experiences and hopes and dreams into one shared space, exploring what it means to be in that place together, the give and take, the push and pull, the compromise, and, ultimately, the parting. Too long analyzing that stuff must be bad for your health."

Keira let out a wry snort. How close Milo was to the truth. All she ever seemed to do was think back over the past, to wonder and mull things over, to leave no stone unturned in her quest for understanding.

"See? Already you're teaching me things," she said.

Milo gazed across the table at her, the skin beside his light blue eyes crinkling as he smiled. They held one another's glance and Keira felt the energy passing between them. Like electricity. But not the type that shocked her and sent her running. The type that felt charged, like a magnet pulling them together.

"Keira," Milo said, his tone sounding all business. "I'm going to ask you whether I'd be able to show you around the city some more tomorrow."

"Oh," Keira said, taken aback by how forthright he was.

She shouldn't have been surprised though. Venla had warned her that there was no messing around when it came to dating. No games. No wasted time. But her resistance was there. Milo seemed, well, kind of perfect, and Keira already knew from experience that there was no such thing. Perfect tended to last for a few weeks at the most before reality came crashing in. And she knew her chances of falling for him were so high as to be inevitable. She'd promised herself she wouldn't do that this time, that she'd complete her assignment on her own, without a man.

"Ah," Milo said then. "I can see that I've misjudged the situation. I'm sorry."

"No," Keira suddenly blurted. "You haven't misjudged it at all. It's me. I'm..." She sighed. "Going through some personal stuff. And then I've got work and..."

Milo shook his head kindly. "It's no problem. Here." He handed her his business card. "There's my number. Perhaps if you change your mind. Even if it's just for another tour? Strictly business."

She took it from him, reading his full name: Milo Nilsson.

"If I change my mind, I promise I'll call," she said.

Milo gave her one quick nod, then stood. "It's been a pleasure to spend time with you, Keira Swanson."

"And you, Milo Nilsson," she replied.

She watched him leave, wondering whether she'd made the right decision, or if she'd just let a potential lover slip through her fingers.

She looked down at the slip of card in her hands. Just a tiny piece of paper that contained the power to potentially change her life. She placed it carefully into her purse.

CHAPTER SEVENTEEN

Keira left the coffee shop, alone, and stood on the streets of Stockholm. Milo's absence felt acute, and for someone whom she'd only met two hours earlier, that sensation seemed quite telling for Keira. Similarly to her meeting with Jossi, she felt like Milo had had some kind of profound effect on her, in spite of him only being in her life for a very short moment of time.

She looked left, then right, taking in the sight of the wide, modern, store-lined street. All her plans for the day seemed to fly out the window. She could hardly concentrate, let alone negotiate her way through an unfamiliar city to contemplate some great works of art. She decided then that instead of visiting any of the locations on her list of sights, she'd learn all about Stockholm through a spot of retail therapy.

She headed right along the street, choosing the direction that would take her away from the palace and Milo. The stores all had their Christmas displays in the window, and it struck Keira then that her only option for buying gifts for her family and friends would be to do so in Sweden. She'd barely have any time in New York on her return.

She came across a store selling cute home furnishings and kitchenware. It seemed like the perfect place to get something for Bryn, a slightly cheeky gift to hint at her sudden domestication at the hands of Felix. She perused the items on the display, her attention drawn to an extensive display of cheese slicers. They were in all different sizes and colors, some even in novelty shapes. Keira looked at them, bemused. Why so many cheese slicers?

A store clerk sidled up to her then. "You're a tourist," she commented.

"Is it that obvious?" Keira said with a chuckle.

"Well, no one from Sweden would look that surprised at the range of cheese slicers on offer. They're a Swedish staple."

Keira raised her eyebrows. "Really?"

The woman nodded. "Oh yes. You will not meet a single person in Sweden who doesn't have at least five of these things. Or…" She leaned over and picked up a small, varnished wooden spoon and handed it to Keira. "…one of these."

"A spoon?" Keira asked, looking at the extremely underwhelming wooden item in her hands.

"It's part of our culture," the store clerk explained. "Bread for breakfast with slices of cheese. And this is for the jam." She tapped the spoon.

"I think this is some kind of elaborate sales ploy," Keira mused. "But it worked. I'll take them both."

She couldn't wait to see the look on Bryn's face when she unwrapped them on Christmas day. You couldn't really get more domestic than a cheese slicer and jam spoon!

The clerk rung up the items at the till and Keira paid, uttered a slightly self-conscious "*Tack!*" and then headed out the store into the streets again.

As she started wandering again, her mind returned to Milo. She wondered whether she'd made the right call shutting him down like that. Another tour would at the very least give her some good material to work with. But she was so afraid of falling for him.

She stopped walking abruptly then. If she didn't want to fall for him, then she wouldn't. It was that simple. She didn't have to be a slave to her heart! Just because she was attracted to him didn't mean she had to avoid him, like she was some kind of creature in heat who couldn't be held accountable for their own actions. She just had to be mature about the whole thing. Professionally aloof. Keep things strictly business. One tour, nothing more.

She took her cell phone out of her purse and found Milo's business card, which she'd put neatly inside the jacket of her notebook. She began typing.

Hi, it's Keira. I've decided a second tour would actually be really helpful for my article. There's a few more questions I'd like to ask you, if you don't mind. Is the offer still open?

She decided against putting a kiss on the end, and reread the message until she was satisfied that it sounded completely un-flirty. Then she hit send.

She didn't have to wait long for a response. Her phone pinged an incoming message so quickly she was certain it couldn't be Milo. But when she looked, it was indeed his name on the screen. She opened the message and read.

Of course. I'd be very happy to see you again. I'll think of a good meeting spot and text you the details in the morning. Can't wait.

Keira immediately felt her cheeks grow warm. He was eager, that much was clear, and regardless of whether she wanted things to be strictly professional or not, it was always nice to be desired.

After the brief communication with Milo, Keira felt buoyant, and she practically skipped her way through the streets of Stockholm. Then, feeling tired from the emotion of the day, she went back to the ship for some quiet writing time.

Sitting in her cozy bed, laptop on her knees, Keira began to free write about her meeting with Milo and what she had learned. Her plan was to write what she wanted to, almost like a diary entry, then shape the passage later into a more usable draft. There were only so many words she could devote to Sweden after all, and just because the meeting with Milo had been *her* favorite of the trip so far, it didn't mean it would be for the readers.

So she typed and typed, losing herself in the memories of the day, the visceral sensations of meeting someone you had such a strong attraction to. By the time she stopped, the sky outside her round window had darkened. She looked back over her writing, surprised at how beautifully she could construct certain sentences when there was passion and drive behind them. And surprised, also, with how evidently her heart yearned for more of Milo.

"You're in charge, brain," she said aloud. "Don't forget that, heart."

She decided against going out for dinner. She was tired, and didn't feel like braving the cold again. Besides, her time on the ship had almost come to an end. Now she wanted to enjoy some of it.

So she had a long soak, put on a face mask and pajamas, did her nails, and watched a cheesy rom-com movie in bed, while picking at the foods in her minibar. It felt great to slob out for fun, rather than out of misery like she had done on Bryn's couch.

Then at some point she fell asleep. And in her dreams, she was wearing a beautiful white silk dress, walking the snowy fields of Sweden to an aisle. At there, waiting for her, was her perfect man. And he looked just like Milo.

*

Keira was woken the next morning by the sound of her phone. It was an incoming text. She came to her senses instantly, remembering how Milo had said he would text her a meeting location in the morning. She grabbed her phone and felt a surge of excitement to see that the message was indeed from him. He'd sent her a location for what he called a "breakfast meeting."

Perfect, Keira thought. *He gets that this is a strictly business thing.*

She leapt out of bed, more enthusiastic than the average person prior to a business meeting. Thanks to all the pampering she'd done last night, she was already looking pretty put together. Her skin was positively glowing, her nails looked like they could have been done professionally, and her hair had a beautiful glossy sheen. She only needed a little bit of makeup to complete her look, and she chose some casual yet smart clothes in order to keep up the pretence of a business meeting. Nothing said business like beige.

As soon as she was ready, she left the ship, wanting to give herself plenty of time to find the cafe. But Milo's directions were so clear she found it right away, and realized she had ten minutes to kill before he was even due to arrive.

She went up to the register to order some coffee. There was a stand of magazines beside the counter, and to her absolute horror, she saw her own face staring back at her. It was the damn *Viatorum* issue again! That cover seemed to be following her everywhere.

"What can I get you?" the barista said, turning her attention to Keira.

"How much is that magazine?" Keira asked.

"The price is on the back," the woman said, and her sentence trailed off. "Wait. Is that YOU?"

Keira's cheeks burned. She grabbed the whole stack of magazines. "I'll buy them all," she muttered.

The barista began ringing them up on the till. "So are you famous then? You must be if you're on the cover of a magazine!"

Keira kept her gaze fixed on the countertop. She was too embarrassed to engage in conversation.

As soon as she'd paid the barista, she grabbed the stack of magazines and headed outside, throwing them in the first trash can she saw. A calmness came over her, a relief to know she wouldn't be subjected, again, to the shame of being the cover star of a magazine in Milo's presence. But then she suddenly realized she should have ripped the covers up. If Milo walked past this particular trash can, he still might see them!

She turned and reached into the garbage, picking up all the magazines, which were now smeared with bits of food. She grimaced, reaching further in for one that had slipped out of her grasp.

With her hands deep in the garbage, she felt a tap on her back. She froze, horrified, then slowly raised herself out of the can, turning slowly to come face to face with Milo.

CHAPTER EIGHTEEN

Keira felt absolutely humiliated. But Milo looked thoroughly amused.

"What *are* you doing?" he asked, laughing.

"I… um… well…" Keira floundered for an excuse. She plucked something out of her mind. "My bracelet. I dropped it."

Milo didn't look convinced. "In the trash?"

"Yeah. And I would have left it but it was a gift from my sister." She gesticulated as she lied, a nervous habit. "Silver. You know? Expensive."

Milo narrowed his piercing blue eyes. "You mean like that bracelet on your wrist?"

Keira's gaze snapped to her hand, held high in the air mid-gesticulation, to see a delicate silver bracelet around it. "Yeah. That one. I found it. Just before you tapped my back."

"Right…" Milo said, tapping his chin. "So you found your bracelet and decided to put it on while still hanging halfway into the trash can?"

Keira smiled through her grimace. "Yup. That's exactly what happened."

Milo nodded, looking skeptically amused.

Keira glanced over her shoulder at the barista who'd commented on her being famous. The last thing she wanted now was to go back in there.

"So I was thinking," she added hurriedly, taking him by the arm and steering him away from the barista's staring eyes through the window, "that we could have breakfast somewhere different. I mean, the food in that place was standard American stuff, and I'd like to sample something more traditional to Sweden."

"Sure," Milo said, shrugging. "If you'd prefer. Did you have anywhere specific in mind?"

"I was hoping you'd know somewhere. How about somewhere on the river? If you can think of a spot."

"Yeah, I can think of somewhere that sells smörgås," Milo said. "This way."

They headed away from the cafe, leaving the incriminating garbage can behind. Soon they reached the riverside. Milo led Keira along the sidewalk and stopped outside a cafe.

"Here," he said. "I've only been here once before. But it fits your criteria, riverside and Swedish menu."

"It's perfect," Keira said, wondering what kind of terrible impression she must be giving off.

They went inside. Milo spoke to the guy behind the bar, ordering, "smörgås" and "stinka."

"You're not pranking me, are you?" Keira asked, warily, as they headed to their seats.

"Not at all," Milo chuckled. "Stinka is ham. You're not a vegetarian, are you?"

Keira shook her head. A moment later the server came over with two wooden boards. On each of them were slices of bread and cheese, little pots of butter, cucumbers, tomatoes, and cold cuts of ham and beef. The server also placed two very strong-looking coffees beside the wood boards.

"Okay, this is a feast!" Keira commented. "What a great way to start the day."

Milo grinned. "I'm glad you approve."

Keira looked away from his enticing smile. *Business, business, business,* she repeated in her mind, as she quickly took her notebook from her bag.

"Shall we get right to it?" she asked.

"Sure," Milo said.

He seemed to have a very easygoing attitude, happy to go along with whatever she suggested.

Keira quickly looked over her notes. She had not even thought to prepare more questions for him. The whole interview aspect of their meeting had gotten lost in her mind since she'd been so focused on the actual meeting part!

"Er... you mentioned equality in relationships last time," she said. "Could you say a bit more about that? Perhaps in relation to marriage?"

No sooner had she said it than she remembered the white wedding dress in her dream, and the perfect man who bore a striking resemblance to the one sitting before her munching on bread.

"Marriage," he said aloud. "It's a tricky one. Can a marriage ever be equal, when the historical foundation of marriage is ownership? A woman belonging to a man? I don't agree with that, so in a way, I can't agree with marriage. That said, I think lots of people these days are pushing the boundaries of what marriage means and why it matters. I respect that transformation. I know a lot of people who marry for legal security in terms of their children and home and inheritance. But that's not particularly romantic, is it? I personally don't know whether I can unpick those two things, the extremely unsexy legal side and the heady romance side. I don't know if they can fully co-exist."

Keira gazed at him as he spoke. His voice was so calming, so soothing. And his answers were so thorough. He clearly thought everything through. It was a charming quality.

Suddenly, Keira realized he'd stopped speaking. She snapped back to attention. "That's fascinating," she said. "I'm guessing that means you haven't been married before? If you have such conflicting opinions on it."

He chuckled and shook his head. "No. Never. I'm very much single at this point in my life."

"And would you marry, if you met someone to whom it was important?"

"Oh, yes, of course!" he said. "I fully appreciate why a partner would want to. Women, in particular, are given less securities in our world than men. If a woman was to, say, give up a year of employment in order to carry and raise my child, it would be only fair and right for her to be legally entitled to whatever money I earned during that period of time. Otherwise, she's sacrificing and I'm gaining. It wouldn't be fair. From that perspective, marriage makes sense to me."

Keira felt herself go off into dreamland again. Milo's views were extremely interesting, not to mention appealing. Who wouldn't want a marriage based on equality? On shared responsibility and respect? If she ever did get married, that would definitely be the way she'd want it to be.

She realized then that her platter of food was sitting uneaten in front of her. She'd been so entranced by Milo and his opinions she hadn't even touched it. She quickly ate some now.

"Oh, this is good," she said. "The cheese is awesome."

"Cheese at breakfast is a very Swedish thing to eat," Milo explained.

Keira thought suddenly of the cheese slicer she'd purchased. "Oh yes! I learned about this yesterday while I was shopping for Christmas gifts. I came away with a cheese slicer and wooden spoon."

Milo began to laugh. "That's most apt. Who's the lucky recipient going to be?"

"My older sister," Keira explained. "Bryn. She's spent the last thirty years on the party scene, never settling, barely even having a relationship, and now suddenly she's in love with this guy who's older than our mother. They're moving in together so I thought I'd get her some tongue-in-cheek kitchen utensils."

Milo chuckled. "That's very funny. I have a sister too. Regina. She's also older. She's an astrophysicist."

Keira raised her eyebrows. "I don't think Bryn would even be able to spell astrophysicist."

They dissolved into easy laughter. Then, once it had subsided, they polished off their respective breakfasts.

"Are you ready for the tour?" Milo asked, once her mug had been drained of coffee.

Keira snapped her notebook shut. The coffee had been so strong she felt her body buzzing with caffeine.

"Yup." She grinned. "Where are you taking me?"

They stood, collecting their jackets from the back of their chairs.

"The Fotografiska museum," Milo told her. "You can probably guess from the name that it's a photography museum."

"I love museums," Keira said, in a dumb, floaty voice.

"I know." Milo smiled.

She felt a stirring in the pit of her stomach, and told her mind, in a very stern voice, to get control over the situation.

*

The Fotografiska museum was, quite simply, amazing. Keira could have spent every weekend of her life from that point forward looking at the incredible photographs without getting tired of it. There was just so much talent on display!

"Photography is my favorite type of art," Milo told her as they walked from one stunning image to the next. "There's a democratization of art when you can make it with technology we all possess. Look, over there is a smartphone exhibition."

"Awesome," Keira agreed. "You seem to know a lot about art."

"My first degree was in art."

"Not history?"

He shook his head. "No. In Sweden our education system is much looser. You can study part time if you want, and all different kinds of subjects. It's not uncommon for people to dip in and out of education for many years, reading around all different types of topics. History and art aren't even that far apart, when you really think about it."

"I guess not," Keira said.

She was enjoying getting glimpses into Milo's mind. He seemed so intelligent. So knowledgeable. Her entire experience with education had been about getting a decent, good-paying job at the end, to take steps away from her childhood struggles. She'd never really thought about studying for the sake of *learning*.

"If you want to stay here," Milo said then, interrupting her thoughts, "I'm very happy to. But I'd really love to show you Stockholm cathedral. It's medieval. Built in 1279."

His enthusiasm was infectious.

"How can I resist?" Keira said.

They walked together to the cathedral, and once inside, Keira was astounded. She couldn't believe how beautiful it was. She tiptoed along the aisle, glancing all about her in wonder.

"There was a royal wedding here not that long ago," Milo told her.

"I can see why," Keira said, twirling on the spot. She was about to say that it was a wedding location fit for a princess, that she would love to marry in a place like that, but she kept her mouth shut, remembering what had happened with Cristiano in France.

"I have one more place to take you," Milo said. "If you still have the energy?"

"That coffee was so strong I don't think it will ever wear off," Keira joked. "So yes, I'm happy to see somewhere else."

"Good," Milo said, smiling.

They left the cathedral and Milo directed Keira toward the canal. There, waiting by a small jetty, was a boat.

"A boat tour," he explained. "Stockholm looks fabulous from the canal."

Keira couldn't help but think of the gondola in Italy, of the way her thigh had pressed against Cristiano's. Milo must have sensed her hesitation, because he looked concerned.

"Is that okay?" he asked. "Or am I making it too much like a date? You were very clear that this was not a date but a business meeting."

Keira couldn't help but laugh. Milo was so forthcoming it was a breath of fresh air. She could really see what Venla meant now about not playing games. Everything was above board, vocalized, and discussed. It was different, but refreshingly so.

"No, it's perfect," she said. "I'm just a little chilly, that's all."

"I anticipated as much," Milo said. He took a blanket from his satchel. "Here, you can wrap this around your shoulders."

Keira took it and wrapped it about her before stepping into the boat. If Milo hadn't literally just made it clear that there was nothing romantic behind his intentions she'd have perceived it to be an extremely flirty and romantic gesture.

He was right though; Stockholm from the vantage of the canal was a sight to behold. For a travel writer, it would have been criminal not to take this trip. Keira was very inspired by all the sights, not to mention the company. She could hardly stop from laughing at all of Milo's comical quips.

The boat guide looked over at them and grinned. "It is so nice," he said, "to see a young couple so in love."

Keira looked at Milo, her eyes wide with shock. He looked back at her coyly, amused, but blushing at the same time. And in that moment, Keira realized she was falling for this guy whether she wanted to or not.

CHAPTER NINETEEN

Keira's mind was spinning by the time she got back to her room that night. Her day with Milo had been fantastic. She'd even planned to meet him again tomorrow. There was no denying that she was falling for him. She didn't even have any of the anxiety she usually felt when getting to know someone new. She felt like she'd known him her whole life.

But the other side of Keira's mind wondered whether that was just what rebounds did to your mind. Could she cope with yet another rebound, of the heady highs and the crushing disappointment that followed? Or should she be throwing caution to the wind? What if Milo was The One, if this was all happening for a reason? What if the universe was trying to tell her something?

As she mulled these thoughts over, toing and froing from one position to the next, she began packing all her stuff. Tonight was her last night on the boat. Tomorrow she would be in a hotel, sleeping in a bed that didn't rock back and forth while she slept. She'd enjoyed the unique experience, but it had been colored somewhat by the drama of Emma's breakup, by her freckled, flirty server, and by that horribly rough day at sea. All things considered, she wasn't that sad about seeing the back of it.

She folded up her sweaters, placing them in her case on top of her shoes. In went her makeup bag, her toiletries, and the carrier bag of Bryn's gifts.

Once she was all packed, she sat down for a final writing session on the boat. Once she'd left, it would be difficult to recreate the experience, and Nina hadn't been particularly complimentary of her passage dedicated to the cruise ship. This, really, was her last chance to capture the essence of the cruise.

She closed her eyes, breathing calmly to feel the ambience, then began to type. But when it came time to mention Milo, she hesitated. She didn't feel like sharing her thoughts or experiences with him yet. For now, she'd skip the specifics. It just didn't seem right. So she reduced him to a mere tour guide, a bit player with a fleeting walk-on role, rather than the significant person she felt he was about to become.

Suddenly, her phone started ringing. Her heart leapt. At first she thought it might be Milo. But when she looked over, she was surprised to see Cristiano's name flashing up at her. Cristiano was calling? Again?

Last time she'd spent so long deliberating over whether to take the call he'd rung off. This time, she wanted to speak to him. She'd given him such mixed signals by texting to say she missed him. And now she wasn't thinking about him like that at all. Her mind had shifted over to Milo. Better to take the call and make it clear, to set the record straight, just like Milo would do.

She answered, afraid as she did so that it would be his new girlfriend calling to attack her. But the voice on the other line was so familiar it felt like lightning striking her heart to hear it again.

"Keira?"

"Cristiano, hey," she replied. She felt suddenly extremely awkward to be speaking to him again, after all those days of misery she'd spent thinking about him, pining for him. "Is everything okay?"

"Yes," he said. He sounded breathless. "This is a bit strange but I was looking through my phone and I saw that you had texted me a few weeks ago. And I hadn't seen the message, but there was a reply from my number."

Keira was surprised to hear that he hadn't even seen the original message.

"Your girlfriend replied," Keira said. "And I'm really sorry. It was a dumb thing to do. I didn't know you'd moved on. I hope I didn't make things awkward between you. That was never my intention."

"Not at all," Cristiano said. "We're not together anymore. She was too controlling, and paranoid, always in my phone."

They were no longer together, Keira thought. That was quite strange. She must have just been a rebound fling after all.

Cristiano continued speaking. "And if anyone should apologize it's me. I shouldn't have cut you out of my life like that. I promised to stay friends with you. But it hurt and I was being childish."

"That's okay," Keira said.

There was a long pause.

"So?" Cristiano said, breaking the awkward silence. "Is it true? Do you miss me?"

Keira felt a tightening in her throat. "I did. I do. But not like that. Not romantically."

"Huh," Cristiano said, sounding disappointed. "So there is no reconciliation on the cards for us then?"

"No," Keira admitted. "I do miss you but we can't be together. That hasn't changed. I'm sorry."

Perhaps if he'd called a week ago, things would have been different. But now, it was too late. Someone else was in her mind, pushing Cristiano completely out of it.

"Okay," Cristiano said simply. He sounded so wounded, like Keira had ripped his soul out all over again.

Before she had a chance to say anything else, the call cut out. Cristiano had gone. Keira felt awful for having given him false hope, and furious at her past self for being so weak and selfish. But things were different now. She had changed. It was time to truly move on.

CHAPTER TWENTY

On waking the next morning, Keira felt sad to know she'd be leaving the cruise ship behind. She'd become quite fond of her little cabin. But she was excited to have a whole eight days to explore Sweden.

And Milo... her brain added before she even had time to stop it.

She washed in the bathroom for the final time, and dressed in the clothes she'd laid out last night; her warmest sweater, jeans, boots, and a jacket. She was about to wheel her case from the cabin when her cell phone beeped.

Keira took the phone from her purse and saw that she'd received a text from Milo. Two days in a row! He really was interested!

Morning, K. Want some help moving your stuff to the hotel? M.

Keira smiled. Milo's text was very *him,* very straightforward and to the point. She liked it, and couldn't help but instinctively compare it to her past partners. Shane only ever communicated in joke form, whereas Cristiano turned everything into a flirting opportunity. Something about the simplicity of Milo's communication really appealed to her.

She sat back on the bed and typed a response.

That would be great!

Within two seconds, her phone pinged his return message.

Good. Because I'm outside.

Keira peered at the message in disbelief. Outside? Outside where? The boat was surrounded on most sides by water!

She stood again, her frown still in place, and wheeled her suitcase out of the cabin. She followed the corridor, emerging out onto deck and taking the exit route from the ship to the outside world. And sure enough, there was Milo, standing beside a small blue car.

Keira's eyes widened. "You really are outside!"

"Yes," Milo said, as if it was obvious. He nodded to the case. "Do you want to put that in the trunk?"

Keira was still too stunned to make sense of the situation. "Uh, yeah," she replied.

She dragged the case around to the back of the car and heaved it up into the open trunk. Milo slammed it down, and then they both walked around the side of the car to their respective seats.

Keira sat down and clipped her belt in place. It felt so strange to be sitting beside Milo in a car like this. Strange, in part, because it felt so normal.

Milo turned the key in the ignition. "I have a whole day of activities planned," he said, looking over at her. "If you have time in your writing schedule."

For the second time that morning, Keira was stunned into silence. She opened her mouth to speak but closed it again immediately. Finally, shaking her head, she managed to utter, "I can find time."

"Cool," Milo said. "Let's get you settled in to your hotel first, shall we?"

"Actually," Keira said, as Milo pulled out of the harbor parking lot and turned onto the main road, "perhaps we could stop for breakfast? I haven't had any yet."

She was getting sick of having nothing but coffee for breakfast. So she was carrying a few extra pounds at the moment. In the grand scheme of things, who really cared!

"Yes, of course," Milo told her. "Swedish again?"

"Absolutely." Keira grinned.

Milo negotiated the roads of Stockholm with ease, driving them up through the city in a northward direction. As they went, the streets seemed to grow narrower, the buildings older and more crooked.

"Are we going back in time?" Keira joked.

Milo laughed, warmly. "In a sense, yes. This part of the city is the oldest, the original part. Some of the buildings around here date back to 1252, the year Stockholm was founded."

Keira looked over at him out the corner of her eye. "You do know you're not on tour duty."

Milo grinned, his eyes still fixed on the round. "Actually, I'm never off it. It's a twenty-four/seven kind of thing for me. If you don't like knowing dates and historical facts, then you're hanging out with the wrong guy." Just then, he abruptly changed topic. "Ah, I've thought of just the place!"

He steered the car into a large multi-story car park. Once he'd found a spot to park, they both got out of the car and headed back to street level. Milo directed Keira around a corner and into an alleyway. It looked absolutely ancient, with all the walls bulging

115

and wonky. Then Milo stopped beside a thick wooden door so low even Keira would have to bend to get through.

"The oldest cafe in Sweden," he said, grinning from ear to ear. "And it serves some very traditional dishes."

"Why am I getting the sense that I'm being tricked?" Keira said, narrowing her eyes suspiciously.

"Not a trick," Milo said, shaking his head while looking quite mischievous.

Skeptical, Keira ducked inside.

The cafe was tiny, with just a few tables crammed in. The ceiling was low, and all the lights had a strange yellow glow to them, as if to emulate oil lamps.

"Welcome to the oldest cafe in Stockholm," the server said.

She was standing behind a large glass counter with all the food items pre-prepared and on display. Keira leaned it to look at what was for sale. Smoked sausage, grilled mackerel, caviar, boiled eggs, and a strange savory cake.

"I'd have the smörgåstårta, if I were you," Milo said, leaning in beside her. He was pointing at the strange layered cakelike thing.

"What's in it?" Keira asked, narrowing her eyes.

"Bread, cream, liver pâté, shrimp, tomato, lemon, salmon, and olives."

Keira identified each different layer as he listed them, and grimaced. "I don't know whether my stomach would be able to cope with something like that!" She looked up at the server. "Could I just have some fruit?"

"Of course," the woman said.

"Chicken," Milo commented. Then, to the server, he added, "I'll have the smörgåstårta."

She smiled and gestured to the empty cafe. "Take a seat wherever you want, I'll bring it over to you."

Milo and Keira headed to a table near the small, crooked window. The alleyway outside was dark from the shadows cast by the tightly positioned buildings and the complete lack of sunshine this morning. There weren't any people around either. Keira reasoned that this must be a very touristy area and since most of them would still be in bed or having breakfast in their hotels, it felt a bit like they had a the city to themselves.

A moment later, the server came over with Milo's savory cake, and a bowl of fruit for Keira. Even though neither had ordered any, she also had two mugs of extremely strong coffee, which she placed on the table before leaving.

Keira peered into her bowl. It was filled with berries, many of which she'd never seen before.

"So what have I got in here then?" she asked Milo. "You'll have to talk me through it."

Milo pointed with his fork at each one. "Lingonberries, bilberries, raspberries, cranberries, buckthorn, crowberry, and cloudberry. And it looks as if you're in luck. There's filmjölk underneath."

"Filmjölk?" Keira repeated, glancing at the strange off-white creamlike substance the berries were lying on. Whatever it was it didn't sound particularly appetizing.

"Sour milk."

"Oh."

She prodded her berries, a little reticent. Milo just chuckled.

"Don't be scared," he said, laughing. "I promise you, it's delicious!"

Finally, Keira took a spoonful. Milo was right. It *was* delicious, if not a little strange. But washed down with some of the exceptionally strong coffee, it was the perfect breakfast for her.

"How's your smorg-a-strata?" Keira asked, looking at the half-eaten, unappealing-looking cake on Milo's plate.

"A little rich," he said. "Could've done without the extra layer of caviar."

Keira pulled a face. Such strong flavors at breakfast seemed very off-putting to her!

They finished eating and drained their coffees. Keira felt the now familiar sensation of caffeine racing through her veins. If there was anything the Swedes did right, it was the strength of their coffee!

When the server came over with the bill, there was a moment of awkwardness. Keira was so used to having her food paid for when she was with a man, that she absent-mindedly didn't even reach for her wallet. But she saw the bill had been split in two and she was expected to cover her half. Just another part of egalitarianism, she thought. Besides, her meals were on *Viatorum*.

"Why don't I get this?" she suggested. "I'll charge it to the company. Call it a breakfast meeting."

Milo laughed and put his credit card back in his pocket. "I'm not about to argue with that."

Keira felt a little surge of power as she footed the bill, knowing it was her hard work and accomplishments that made it possible. She wondered for the first time if being an independent woman didn't have to involve sacrificing love. At least, not in a Scandinavian country.

Fueled for the morning, they left the restaurant and headed back to the parking lot. As they climbed the steps to the second floor where Milo had parked, he seemed in very good spirits. He was enthusiastic at the best of times, but now with a cup of strong coffee in him he was borderline hyper!

"You're in a good mood," Keira commented.

"Well, I've always wanted to go there," he explained. "For the history of it, you know?"

"You never did before?" Keira asked, surprised. "But it's perfect for you! It's like a museum in a cafe."

He laughed and shook his head. "Exactly. But it's that typical tourist thing, isn't it? You never visit the tourist attractions when you live somewhere."

"I guess," Keira agreed, thinking of all the New York City locations she'd never visited. "Well, I'm glad I could assist."

They reached the car and got back in. Milo drove the short distance to Keira's hotel. From the outside, it looked like a very small B&B. The building itself was old, thankfully, and not one of the new hotels she'd seen the other side of the city, and it was situated down a quiet, tree-lined road.

Keira took her trunk from the back, noting the stark difference between Milo, who didn't even think to chivalrously help her, and Cristiano, who would have died of shame had he not taken the burden of heavy lifting off her dainty feminine shoulders. It was impossible to work out which approach she preferred. It had been so drummed into her through her entire life that men should help, that her instinct was to think Milo was a little rude for not coming to her aid. But was that just the cultural differences at play? Would Venla or Anita think twice about carrying their own luggage?

Milo followed Keira inside. At the reception desk, Keira checked in, collected her key, then wheeled her case along the corridor to her new room. It was lovely inside, a small room decorated with dark green wallpaper and walnut-wood furniture. She deposited her case against the wall, where black-and-white images depicting horse-drawn trams hung.

"Come on, history nerd," Keira said to Milo. "When did the tram system stop being horse drawn?"

"It was electrified in 1901," he said, without missing a beat.

Keira laughed. Milo looked pleased with himself.

"There'll be plenty more facts for you when we do the tour today," he added. "Today is all about Vikings."

"It is?" Keira said. That was the first she'd heard of it.

Milo grinned his mischievous grin. "Yes. And in fact, we'd better hurry." He checked his watch. "The minivan will be here in a few minutes!"

Minivan? Keira thought as she followed him, bemused, out of the room.

They left the B&B together. It was a gray, cold day, and Keira fiddled with the belt of her jacket. Milo didn't wait for her. He rushed ahead, all the way to the end of the narrow street to a small square of grass that had nothing more than a bench upon it. And there, parked beside the green, to Keira's utter surprise, was a minivan with the Swedish flag emblazoned across it.

"What on earth..." Keira muttered.

From the van's open doors, Milo waved, beckoning her eagerly to hurry. Keira jammed her cold hands deeply into her pockets and strode over to join him.

"What is going on?" she asked, surprised and amused in equal parts.

"We're going on a Viking tour!" Milo said enthusiastically. "It's just a short trip, but it will take us to some of the most important places of Viking significance around the outskirts of Stockholm."

"You mean to say you're leaving the touring up to someone else?" Keira joked. "But surely you already know all the facts?"

"Oh, I do," he said, grinning. "But I never get tired of it. Anyway... surprise!"

Keira felt the side of her mouth twitch up. Milo was... well, a bit zany. But she liked it. She liked his unapologetic enthusiasm for all things historic. He had a strong sense of self, and something about that was incredibly appealing.

He stepped up on board and Keira laughed to herself before following. Deep down inside her stomach, she had a feeling that today was going to be a very strange day indeed!

*

The minivan headed north, leaving the bustling city behind and venturing out into the natural beauty of the Swedish countryside. Which, of course, was the perfect time for the weather to turn drizzly and the windows to fog up.

"Welcome aboard," their guide said. He was precisely the gray-haired, corduroy-clad man she'd been expecting Milo to be back in the museum. "The first stop on our Viking tour is the town of Täby.

119

Here, we'll take a brief stop to look at the ancient stone circles, at the sight of Viking parliament."

Keira looked over at Milo, whose eyebrows shot up with excitement. She couldn't help but laugh. The way he got excited about history reminded her of a Labrador being thrown its favorite ball.

After a short time, the minibus slowed to a halt. Keira defogged the window with her sleeve and peered out. Far from being the sparse country village she'd been expecting, Täby was a modern, bustling town, filled with new architecture. Keira couldn't help but feel a little disappointed. It seemed as if all the history had been eradicated.

"Where's all the Viking stuff?" she asked Milo.

"Oh, it's coming," he said eagerly. "Just you wait!"

They exited the bus and followed their guide across the muddy ground toward a lake. Surrounding it, in a circular route, were several stones, each one approximately four feet high. It was, Keira had to admit, pretty awesome. Each rock had its own unique, intricate patterns and letterings carved into it. The whole area felt very mystical. Milo, of course, was over-awed.

"Aren't they just spectacular?" he enthused.

"Do you know what they're for?" she asked.

"They're signposts," he explained. "They list all the architectural achievements of Viking elders. Sort of huge proclamations."

"You mean like, 'hey, I built a bridge'?" Keira asked.

"Precisely!" Milo said. "Jarlabanke Bridge, to be exact." He pointed ahead to a small, crumbling stone bridge. "It's nine hundred years old!"

He said it like it was the most incredible thing in the world, and Keira couldn't help but grin.

Together, they followed the circuitous route, taking in each of the ancient stones as well as two small churches on the way. It was quite a small site, and they were back at the bus in less than half an hour.

They climbed back on, grateful to be out of the drizzle, and headed on to their next location; an archaic Viking settlement called Granby.

"This settlement dates back to 400 AD," Milo told Keira as they pulled up in Granby.

Just a moment later, the tour guide said exactly the same thing. Keira laughed, thoroughly amused.

They left the warmth of the bus for another whistle-stop tour of crumbling stone monuments, dilapidated buildings, and tiny pathways. It was, in Keira's opinion, a little underwhelming, especially since the rain made it difficult to see, and the mud slopped at her ankles. But Milo's extreme levels of enthusiasm made up for it, and she couldn't help but get swept up into the moment with him.

Their next stop was a gorgeous little church called Orkesta Kyrka. Inside were some beautiful murals.

"When were these painted then?" Keira whispered to Milo. She was certain he couldn't possibly know such an obtuse fact.

"Twelfth century," he whispered back.

"The frescoes you see here have been preserved since the twelfth century," their guide then announced.

Keira shook her head in disbelief.

The bus traveled on through some gorgeous countryside before stopping at Sweden's oldest town, Sigtuna. It was a beautiful place, filled with tiny streets, boutique stores, and, of course, Viking relics. Milo whizzed around like a kid in a candy store.

Keira caught sight of a gift store that was stocked with traditionally silly Viking memorabilia.

"Can we go inside?" she asked Milo.

"Of course," he replied, looking almost confused that she'd even ask.

Keira went first, Milo following. The store was warm, which was a welcome relief from the icy rain, and very small. It took them about two seconds to peruse the shelves. The store stocked a combination of typical gift-shop stuff—erasers, pencils, and keychains—as well as some more elaborate touristy things.

"My mom would love this," Keira joked, putting a Viking hat on. She looked at herself in the small mirror. She looked ridiculous!

"You should get her one for Christmas," Milo suggested.

He took one from the shelf and placed it on his head. Side by side in the mirror, they looked thoroughly absurd, and Keira couldn't stop laughing. In the end, she bought not just one hat, but three, so she and Milo could wear one each, and she could take one home to Mallory.

They headed back to the bus in their matching Viking hats. Their tour guide raised his eyebrows in disdain when he saw them. He was the type of serious man who'd never be seen dead in such a silly item of headwear, Keira thought. The complete opposite of Milo, who had a sense of humor and didn't take himself particularly seriously at all.

121

"Would you like me to drop you off at the hotel?" the tour guide asked.

"Please," Keira said.

"Actually," Milo said, addressing Keira, "I was wondering if I could take you out for dinner? And just to be crystal clear, it would be a date."

Keira couldn't help but laugh at his complete transparency. She had to admit, their whole day had practically been a date. From the moment he'd appeared outside the boat this morning, they'd been on their first date. It would be stupid to pretend otherwise.

Yet still, with it made so blatant, Keira hesitated. There was no way of tricking herself into believing it was for work or research purposes. This time, dinner with Milo would be solely for romance.

Is it a rebound? she wondered. Was she setting herself up for disappointment? But then, how would she ever know if she didn't take the chance?

"I'd like that a lot," Keira said finally.

"Great." Milo grinned.

As they got back on the bus, she swallowed hard. The decision had been made. There was no turning back now.

CHAPTER TWENTY ONE

After they'd driven back to Stockholm, the minivan pulled up outside a very fancy-looking restaurant.

"This isn't where we're going, is it?" Keira asked Milo.

"Yes," he said. "Is that okay?"

Other than the fact that they were arriving in a gaudy van with the bright Swedish flag on the side, Keira had rain-drenched hair and mud-splattered clothes.

"Um, I would've liked to have gotten changed first," she admitted. "It looks quite fancy!"

Milo shrugged. "Fancy? Not really. It's a famous restaurant but it's not particularly posh. You can head back to the hotel to change if you want."

Keira peered out at the rain and the darkening gray sky. She sighed. "No, it's okay."

They left the van, thanking their guide for the wonderful trip, and headed inside the restaurant. Keira self-consciously smoothed down her frizzy flyaway hairs as they stepped inside.

She relaxed a little once she was inside. Milo was right, the restaurant had a very relaxed vibe. It wasn't just lots of couples in fancy clothes on dates, but instead, groups of loud, chatty friends. She noticed also that almost everyone was eating meatballs.

"Is this place famous for its meatballs?" she asked Milo, suddenly enthusiastic. "I haven't eaten any yet."

"Well then, you're going to love it! This place has the reputation for the best meatballs in Sweden."

They were shown to a table by a server who handed them a menu that listed five different meatball dishes and nothing more. Keira opted for the meatballs in cream sauce, while Milo chose a tomato sauce.

"Do you drink wine?" Milo asked.

Keira nodded, though she was anxious to drink in his company. Her last few experiences with alcohol had been a little messy. And wine reminded her too much of Cristiano. She didn't want any comparisons.

"Actually, is there a traditional Swedish alcohol I could try?" she asked.

"Brännvin," Milo told her.

"What's that?"

"It's pretty much vodka. But it's flavored with herbs."

Keira wasn't sure vodka was a better option than wine, but she did want an authentic experience. "I'll have that."

Milo seemed surprised with her boldness, but he ordered two glasses nonetheless.

"So, I'm aware I haven't really asked you anything more for my article," Keira said, leaning across the table. "I've gotten a bit caught up in the moment."

Milo chuckled. "Well, may I ask that you don't start now? We're on a date, remember. Strictly no work conversation."

"Oh, wow, okay," Keira replied, giggling and holding her hands up in a truce position. "But I don't know what else to talk about other than my work. My job is my life!"

"What about your family?" Milo suggested. "You've mentioned a sister and a mom. Are you close?"

"We are," Keira nodded. "It's only ever been the three of us. I mean, we wind each other up a lot, but we have each other's backs. Most the time. What about you? Are you close to your family?"

"I am," he said, nodding. "We're all massive nerds, which helps. My dad, Nils, loves to travel. He's been all over the world, and our house is full of cultural artifacts from far flung countries. My mom, Yolanta, is a union representative. Her life is politics and protests and workers' rights."

"She sounds awesome."

"She is," he confirmed, nodding. "They both are. And my sister is like the smartest woman in the world."

Keira could tell just from the way his eyes twinkled as he spoke that he loved his family very dearly.

"I have a question for you," he said then.

"Oh?" Keira asked.

"Why *were* you digging in the trash?"

Keira let out a loud, embarrassed giggle. "I can't say. It's work related."

"I can waive that rule for this one specific thing," Milo replied, laughing.

Keira could feel her cheeks getting pink. She really didn't want to bring up the cover. But this was Milo. There was no reason to feel self-conscious in front of a self-professed nerd.

"My magazine was on sale in the coffee shop and I didn't want you to see it, so I bought all the copies and threw them in the trash."

He looked at her, bemused. "Then you changed your mind and wanted to get them back out?"

Keira sighed. "No. I wanted to rip them up. Because…" She squirmed in her seat. "Well, I'm on the front cover."

Milo's eyes widened instantly. "Really?" he exclaimed. "Haha! That's amazing! I *have* to see this."

Keira buried her face in her hands. "No, no, no. It's so embarrassing. I'm posing with my ex. It's this black-and-white Parisian movie theme."

"Ah, now I get it," Milo commented. "You didn't want me to see your ex."

Keira peered out her fingers. "No."

"Why? Was he grotesque?"

"No!" Keira laughed. "It just ended quite abruptly and it's still painful."

"Can I ask what happened?"

Keira didn't really want to address this topic with Milo, but he asked so politely and seemed so genuine she felt herself opening up. "It was moving too fast. He proposed. I said no. I wasn't ready to settle down yet."

"Wow," Milo replied. "I'm so sorry. That must have been a very tough breakup."

Keira realized there wasn't even the smallest hint of jealousy in his tone. She felt herself relaxing even more. "It was… an intense relationship. It came off the back of another romance—a boyfriend who broke it off suddenly when his father passed. So I thought he was a rebound but I fell for him hard. And then it ended too. It's been emotionally very taxing."

"It sounds like your heart has been through a lot," Milo said. "Is that why you hesitated when I asked for a date?"

She nodded, slowly, cautiously. She wasn't sure how much she should be telling him. "Let's just say it's been a crazy year for me. Everything's changed. Work. Home. Partner. Everything."

"I'll try not to be too pushy then," Milo said. "Which will be hard, because I like you a lot."

Keira blushed. His candidness still took her by surprise. "I like you too," she admitted.

Just then, their meatballs and vodka arrived, putting a natural end to the conversation, much to Keira's relief. The food looked and smelled amazing, and she licked her lips in anticipation. Milo picked up his little shot glass.

"Let's toast to the future," he said. "And whatever she may hold."

Keira, feeling suddenly overwhelmed with possibilities, raised her glass and clinked it against his. "To the future."

In unison, they downed their vodka shots.

*

A Viking tour and dinner weren't the only surprises Milo had for Keira. After eating, he suggested yet another location.

"The ice bar," he said. "Have you ever been?"

Keira felt a little merry from the vodka shot. "No. Is it cold?"

He gave her a look as if to say the answer to her question ought to have been obvious. "Yes, it's cold," he confirmed. "I mean, it's a bar made of ice. The clue is in the name! But they'll give us thick coats to wear."

Keira was feeling adventurous, so she threw caution to the wind and agreed.

They arrived at the ice bar and were given fur-lined ponchos and gloves to wear. For the second time that day, the two of them looked utterly ridiculous together. But Keira didn't care. Looking like a fool in front of Milo didn't concern her at all.

Once dressed, they were led down a staircase into a dark room. Keira gasped. Not just because of how freezing it was, but because of how stunningly beautiful the interior was. There were ice sculptures everywhere. Chandeliers made of ice. Ice fountains. And even the tables and chairs were made of ice.

"Would you like a drink?" Milo asked.

"I'll get them," Keira said boldly.

She went up to the ice bar and ordered two vodka cocktails, then returned to their ice table and handed Milo his. Just as they had in the restaurant, they clinked their glasses together before downing the shot in unison. Keira remember the shot she'd shared with Rob at Shelby's party, and realized how utterly opposite this experience was with Milo. Here, she felt completely at ease. Milo wasn't the type of guy who'd accuse her of leading her on, of flirting, of owing him something. He was smart and gentle and easygoing. He was everything she'd ever wanted in a man.

She felt the warm alcohol worming into her stomach. The contract between the freezing environment and burning alcohol was quite interesting.

"Thank you for today," she said, leaning into Milo, feeling confident from the liquor. "It's been a really great day."

"I'm glad you've enjoyed yourself. Thanks for letting my inner geek go wild."

Keira laughed. Milo seemed to have a way about him that made her feel carefree. There was no pretence with him, no image he was trying to project. He was just himself, and it felt very appealing.

"So, a little FYI," Milo said. "After these drinks, I'm going to offer to walk you back to your hotel. And if you say yes, I would then like to kiss you on the doorstep. I think it would be a fitting location for our first kiss. How do you feel about that?"

Keira burst out laughing. She found his simple honesty so charming.

"I'd like that a lot," she said. "But I don't think our first kiss should be there, personally."

"No?" Milo asked, smirking. "Where would you prefer it to be?"

"Well, I was thinking that this crazy ice bar might be a good location," she replied.

"You mean right now?" Milo asked, blinking in shock.

Keira nodded. "Right now."

Then she leaned forward and placed her lips softly against Milo's.

She hadn't known what to expect from kissing Milo, but she certainly had not anticipated the sensation of fireworks exploding through her body or the zap of electricity now racing through her veins. Everything fit perfectly, and Keira felt an enormous surge of lust build inside of her.

She pulled back, gazing into Milo's eyes, stunned and breathless.

"Come back with me," she said. "To the hotel. Right now."

"But what about our drinks?" Milo said.

"I don't care about our drinks," Keira said.

She grabbed his hand. Feeling more powerful and in control than ever, Keira led Milo from the ice bar. Her desire to know him inside out was stronger than it had been for any man before in her life.

CHAPTER TWENTY TWO

Keira woke in unfamiliar surroundings and with a groggy headache. She peered at the room in the dull blue light and fragments of memory returned to her. Of course, she wasn't staying on the ship any longer, she'd moved to a hotel. Milo had helped her. Milo!

She say bolt upright as memories of their lovemaking last night returned to her. But the other side of the bed was empty, though the covers were disturbed. It was then that Keira smelled coffee, mixing with the aroma of bread and cheese. She looked over at the dresser. There was a bunch of flowers upon it, lying beside a coffee pot on a silver tray. Two open sandwiches were also on the tray.

Just then, the en suite door opened and steam rushed out. Through the steam emerged Milo, naked and glistening wet.

"You're awake." He grinned.

Keira didn't know where to look. She averted her gaze from his naked physique. "Did you go out and get breakfast?" she asked, shell-shocked by it all.

"Yeah. Thought I'd let you sleep. You seemed exhausted. Shall I pour you a coffee?"

"Thanks," Keira mumbled, still not sure where to look.

She bunched the covers up under her armpits, feeling suddenly very vulnerable. In the cold light of day, she could see now that she'd moved far too quickly with Milo. She'd slept with him! After one date! This kind of rebound experience was exactly what she'd been trying to avoid. And now he'd gone to great lengths to fetch her breakfast and flowers. What a mess. She was going to have to break another heart now.

Milo came over then with the tray and coffee. He placed it by Keira's feet, smiling broadly.

"Fun night, huh?" he said, wiggling his eyebrows and handing her a mug.

"Uh-huh," she replied.

Milo paused. His smile faded. "Are you okay?"

"I'm fine," Keira told him, but deep down she was not. Deep down she wanted Milo to leave so she could have the space to sort out the mess that was her mind.

"No you're not," Milo commented. "You can be honest with me, you know that."

Keira clutched the steaming mug of coffee. Milo had always been straight with her. It would be unfair to hide the truth from him. "I just feel like things are moving too quickly."

"Ah," Milo said. He looked down. "But I didn't push you, did I? Last night happened of your volition."

"Yes," she confirmed, and his face looked more at ease. "I just think I was acting too hasty. We haven't known each other very long."

Milo nodded. He looked downcast, but understanding. He stood and began to dress.

"I'm sorry," Keira said, feeling terrible.

"Don't be sorry," Milo told her. He didn't seem mad at all. Just a bit unhappy. "I asked you to be honest and I appreciate that you were. I just feel a little embarrassed." He looked over at the flowers. They seemed to suddenly be an overblown, misjudged gesture. He finished dressing and turned back to face her. "I'll give you some space. But call me later if you want." He shrugged.

"Okay," Keira said meekly.

She watched Milo leave the room, feeling horrible but at the same time relieved.

*

Keira readied herself for the day, then headed out of the B&B. A day of sightseeing on her own was exactly what she needed to calm her spinning mind. She was falling behind with work as well, and it would be good for her to spend some time doing what she loved most, writing.

She decided she'd visit the most popular museum in Stockholm, the Vasa museum, which housed an old shipwreck. As she strolled the streets, heading toward the royal parkland, Djurgården, where the museum was located, she felt terrible about Milo. He must be so confused by her, by all the toing and froing. But Keira couldn't help it. She was never able to work out what she wanted. There were so many influences in her life, so many voices telling her what she should do and when, that it was impossible to pick out her own desires from the din.

She reached the museum and went inside. It was very busy, with lots of children running excitedly around. Keira could fully see why. The enormous seventeenth-century warship hung centrally in the large room, with space to walk beneath it as well as around it.

Keira stared up at it, feeling the history seeping into her. She wished that Milo could have been there to whisper little facts in her ear, about how it sank in the waters of Stockholm in 1628, and how it spent exactly three hundred and thirty-three years lying on the seabed before being salvaged, restored, and re-homed in the museum.

There was so much more to the museum than just the ship, and Keira soon found herself lost in all the exhibitions. They covered everything from life aboard the ship, the salvaging process, information on the royal family at the time, war, how the shipyard worked, and the lives of seventeenth-century women. It was fascinating.

When she stopped for lunch, Keira felt like her mind had been saturated with information. She'd been right about needing some time alone, and some distraction from her thoughts, but as she sat now, in the museum cafe, sipping coffee, it all came crashing back at her. Why did she struggle so much with relationships? Why did she sabotage everything good? Why was she always so goddamn indecisive?

On the table opposite, Keira noticed an elderly couple. She stood and walked over to them.

"Excuse me," she said. "I'm sorry to disturb you. I'm a writer and I'm trying to learn about love, about how different cultures approach love. May I ask you some questions?"

"Of course," the elderly woman said, gesturing to the seat. She patted her husband's hand. "Like most old people, Ulrich and I love nothing more than to talk about ourselves."

Keira laughed and took a seat opposite them. "Thank you. Have you enjoyed the museum today?"

It was Ulrich who spoke. "I used to be a naval officer. We must come to this place at least twice a year, don't we, Heidi?"

"We alternate," Heidi added. "Between Vasa and the maritime museum. We love them both." Then she lowered her voice. "Although we also go to the Abba museum occasionally, as a special treat."

Keira smiled. It looked as if she had two more history buffs on her hands!

"May I ask, if you don't mind, how long you've been together?"

Her experience in the Nordic countries thus far had taught her not to be so presumptuous to assume an elderly couple were married.

"We married in the seventies," Heidi explained. "The children came along quite soon after. They're grown up now, with their own families."

"So you've successfully navigated the waters of a long marriage," Keira stated. "What's your secret?"

Ulrich's eyes twinkled. "Independence."

"Oh?" Keira said. It wasn't what she'd been expecting to hear.

Heidi chuckled. "Yes. That's probably it. We never compromised our independence. Ulrich had his navy duties, so he'd be away from home a lot. I had my own business making dresses, and I sometimes needed to tour the country for fashion shows. There was never a presumption that I'd stay home and look after the kids when he was with the navy. If I had to go, I had to go. My work was just as important as his."

"Who looked after the kids then?" Keira asked. "When you were both away?"

"Family," Heidi explained. "We were very lucky to live close by to aunts, uncles, grandparents. There was never a shortage of helping hands."

Keira nodded. She wondered how well things would have gone for the pair had there not been family nearby. "So, keeping that autonomy was the most important thing, in your eyes?"

"Certainly," Ulrich said. "There were times when I would be home, but it would coincide with Heidi traveling for a show. I never ever expected her to drop everything just to see me. I made my decision to do a job that took me away from home and she respected that, despite the sacrifices. If I'd not done the same for her it would have been, well, truly unfair. She would have resented me."

"And anyway," Heidi added. "Absence makes the heart grow fonder. We managed to keep that honeymoon phase going for a good decade!"

Ulrich laughed.

Keira watched them, genuinely moved by the love they shared and the respect that was so important to the success of their marriage.

"What about now?" she asked. "I assume there's less traveling for both of you now. Is that spark still there?"

"Well, now," Ulrich said, "I spend a lot of time in the shed building model ships."

"And I spend a lot of time in my workshop making clothes," Heidi added. "I haven't retired yet, although I have slowed down considerably."

Keira was amazed. "Are there still days you don't see each other?" she asked, surprised.

"Oh yes," Ulrich said. "But then there are plenty of dates. Like today."

"It's just how it works for us," Heidi explained. "We want to respect one another's needs. We compromise without sacrificing our own. No one appreciates a martyr, really, do they?"

Keira finished writing down Heidi's closing statement, then shut her notebook. "Thank you so much for speaking to me. It's been truly illuminating."

*

Keira left the museum and searched in her bag for her phone. She found it and called Bryn. Her sister answered quickly.

"How's Sweden?" she asked, enthusiastically.

"Not what I expected," Keira confessed.

"How so?"

"I can't explain it. Everyone is so... honest. It's like every conversation you have is some kind of philosophical therapy session."

"That sounds tiresome," Bryn replied.

"It's not. It's kind of amazing. There's no guessing. What you see is what you get."

Bryn's pause seemed like the equivalent of a shrug. "And work? Have you been getting much done?"

"Enough," Keira said. "But Elliot's demands are messing with my head."

"What's he demanding this time?" Bryn asked, sounding exasperated on Keira's behalf.

"Remember how I told you this trip was all about not rebounding? Well, he wanted me to put myself out there still, to date men, or else there wouldn't be enough romance in the article. And..."

"One thing led to another?" Bryn guessed.

"Yes," Keira sighed. "Why am I so weak?"

"Who told you that falling for someone was weak?" Bryn contested.

Keira rubbed her weary eyes. "I'm such a mess, Bryn. I don't know how you used to do it. You always moved so seamlessly from one guy to the next. But I feel like I give too much away to every guy I'm with, and it's exhausting. I can never tell if I'm rebounding, or really falling in love. When I met Shane I thought he was the

132

One. But then Cristiano came along and he seemed even better. And now there's Milo."

"Milo," Bryn repeated. "Sexy name."

"I know. And he's like this absurdly gorgeous history nerd. And he's so forthright. There's no games, no messing around. Everything is straightforward. Last night, I was so certain I wanted to take things to the next step. But then this morning I got cold feet and sent him packing." Keira took a deep breath.

Bryn paused for a long time. Then finally she spoke. "Hon, I don't mean to be rude or anything, but have you ever thought that maybe you just overthink everything?"

Keira pursed her lips. "I'm a writer, of course I do."

"Right," Bryn said. "Because you know the reason I was able to move seamlessly from one guy to a next was because I just listened to my instincts. I could be in love with a guy for forty-eight hours, then just wake up on Monday morning and not be anymore, break it off, and go about my life. I never agonized over anything."

"You never thought you might be letting someone go you shouldn't?"

"No. Because if I shouldn't let them go, I wouldn't. I'm just saying trust yourself more. Don't shut yourself off because you think you should, or because you have some kind of idea in your head about what you should or shouldn't be doing. Just listen to your gut and stop overthinking it."

"That's like asking a fish not to swim, Bryn," Keira joked wryly. "I can't not think."

"Well, then try writing," Bryn suggested. "Get all your thoughts on paper and out of your head. Write for your eyes only, without a perceived audience or boss looking over your shoulder all the time. Then maybe you'll have some space left in there!"

Keira thought that was actually pretty good advice from Bryn.

"Also," her sister continued, not yet finished, "send me a picture of this guy. I can tell you whether he's worth the effort or not."

"Bye, Bryn," Keira laughed, ending the call.

It was too cold to write in a park, so Keira stopped into the next coffee shop she came across. Thanks to Milo's breakfast coffee, she was still feeling caffeinated up, but she ordered another one anyway. Then she took Bryn's advice and began to write, pouring her heart and soul onto the page.

She wrote about Milo, about how much she struggled to decide if a relationship was a rebound or something more. She wrote about the way past relationships affected current ones, how every decision she made seemed to be in relation to Shane or Zach or Cristiano. She wrote about how she couldn't even be sure that the guys she fell for weren't just relative to the one prior, as though her body instinctively craved something different. Then finally she wrote about the Swedish culture as a whole, about what it had taught her about love and marriage.

When she finished writing, she realized the sky had darkened and the coffee shop was shutting up around her. She blinked, dazed, and shut her notebook. Her hand was cramped. She headed back to her B&B, alone.

CHAPTER TWENTY THREE

Keira felt surprised the next morning not to be awoken by a text from Milo. She'd had three days in a row of him being there in some capacity first thing, and it felt like something was missing. But she also knew that Milo had left the ball in her court. He was too respectful to go against her wishes for space.

She got out of bed, wondering what to do with her day. She'd ended up typing up and editing some of the words she'd written yesterday, melding them with the interview with Heidi and Ulrich, and had sent them to *Viatorum,* which would probably mean an email of edits would be coming her way soon. She decided to have a quiet day, sticking close to the hotel so she could dash back to work on the article.

She washed and dressed for the day. It was another cold, gray one, and by the looks of the sky it would possibly even snow today, so she made sure to wrap up well. Then she put her laptop and notebook in her purse. Her hand still hurt from all the writing she'd done yesterday, so she'd have to switch to typing for today at least. She'd take her laptop out more often if it didn't feel like lugging bricks around all day.

She was just about ready to leave for her morning dose of Swedish caffeine when her phone rang. She saw that it was *Viatorum* and answered the call, as always, with a sense of trepidation.

"KEIRA!" Elliot exclaimed on the other end. "Your most recent passage is GOLD!"

"Oh," Keira replied, a little startled. "Well, thanks." Writing the first draft as if no one would ever read it was clearly a good approach. But she hadn't thought it was *that* good. She still hadn't included anything about Milo in her submissions, so as far as Elliot knew she had not yet fulfilled his requirement of going on a date.

"So what's going to happen?" Elliot continued. "Between you and the Swedish guy?"

Keira frowned then. Was Elliot some kind of mind reader? She hadn't sent Elliot anything about Milo, other than a vague passing reference to a museum guide. Then a horrible sensation overcame her. Had she inadvertently attached the passage she'd written about

135

him, the one that had been for her eyes only? The thought horrified her. She hadn't even gotten Milo's consent yet!

Stalling for time, she quickly checked her emails and saw, with dawning mortification, that she had indeed attached not just the passage regarding the Vasa museum, but also the part that had been for her eyes only, about Milo and her confusion over him!

She gritted her teeth. Including Milo in her article had not been her intention at all. Without having spoken to him about it fully, it felt intrusive for anyone else to have viewed that level of personal detail.

"I don't think that bit should make the final cut," she said quickly.

"Why not?" Elliot said. "It's the best your writing has ever been."

Keira floundered for an explanation. "I haven't gotten his express consent yet to be in the article. And I'm supposed to not rebound, remember?"

"Ah, screw it," Elliot replied. "So what if a focus group says they want to see you independent? You do romance, Keira, and you do it well. We'll turn Meredith into the Anti-Romance Guru if that's what has to happen. You stick to what you do best."

Keira let out an exhalation. No wonder she was always in such a perpetual state of confusion. It must be filtering down from Elliot! And his casual attitude toward not having obtained consent irked her.

"So?" he pressed. "What's next for you and Mr. Hunk?"

Keira sat back on the bed, her mind spinning. She felt dizzy from the mistake she'd made, and didn't know now how to backtrack, how to undo whatever she'd unleashed. Indeed, it seemed impossible now. Elliot's thirst had been quenched for something and her job was to deliver it. She didn't know what to do.

"I don't know!" she exclaimed, the frustration audible in her tone. "I wasn't supposed to be writing another love story so I cooled things off with him. The narrative wouldn't make sense if we added it in so let's just leave it." She added, desperately, "I mean, I didn't get his consent beforehand so I really don't feel comfortable putting any of that stuff in the final draft."

But Elliot seemed to have heard only one thing she'd said, because he commented, "You cooled things off because of the magazine?" He sounded surprised, as if it had never occurred to him that Keira might actually be bending her life to suit his whims, even though she'd said it expressly to his face.

Suddenly, it all got too much for Keira.

"YES!" she exclaimed, growing increasingly more annoyed.

"Well, don't do that. I mean, we thought you wanted a break so the whole no-rebound thing was to take the pressure off. But if you've found a guy, jeez, don't let me stand in the way! Keira, I'd give anything for my own Milo. He sounds like a treasure. Arrange another date and get that approval, okay? The world NEEDS to read this!"

Keira took three very slow, deep breaths. She felt like she could explode with fury.

"Elliot, if you want me to make my own mind up about Milo, then stop giving me your opinion. Okay? Stop telling me I should fall in love, and then I shouldn't fall in love, and then that I should. It's driving me crazy. If I call Milo, I'll do it for me, and I won't write about it for *Viatorum*. AND, while I'm at it, can you STOP printing that cover! It's everywhere I go! I can't stand it!"

As soon as her tirade was over, Keira felt awful. She'd never spoken so abruptly to Elliot. His long silence made her stomach churn with anguish.

"Goodbye, Keira," Elliot said, simply.

The call ended. Keira sat there, staring at her cell in her hand, wondering what she'd just done.

*

It took her awhile to recover from her outburst. She felt drained from the expulsion of emotion, and needed a Swedish-strength coffee more than ever. She grabbed her bag and headed out of the B&B, stopping in the first cafe she found.

She ordered coffee and took her position by the window. As she sat, she thought about Milo, about whether she should call him. Whether she should bend to Elliot's demands and get his consent to put him in her article, even though she was ambivalent at best, and would prefer to keep that stuff private, just between them, if she could. Her mind was too clouded with Elliot's opinions to sort through the muddle of thoughts. Calling Milo was exactly what he wanted, and she didn't much feel like doing him any favors at this point in time.

When her coffee arrived, she took a deep sip, letting the caffeine help focus her mind. But even coffee couldn't bring her any clarity.

Then her phone began to ring, and with horror, Keira realized it was *Viatorum* calling again. Was Elliot ringing back to give her a

137

piece of his mind? To chastise her for blowing up at him like that? She half wanted to ignore the call, but she knew it would just make everything worse.

Swallowing her anxiety, she picked up her phone and answered the call.

"Yes...?" she said in a small, terrified voice.

"Hey, it's Nina. How's it going?"

Keira blinked with surprise. Not only was she not expecting to hear Nina's voice, but she sounded very much like the old Nina, the friend that Keira missed, rather than the editor she'd grown to sort of dislike.

"What do you mean?" Keira asked, uncertain.

"What do you mean what do I mean?" Nina laughed. "I just asked how you were."

Keira stayed silent, her mind whirring. "But why?"

"Why? Because I'm interested? We're friends, aren't we?"

Keira ran her fingers around the rim of her coffee mug. She felt suddenly inspired by Milo's candor, and replied, boldly, "Actually, I'm not always sure we are."

There was a pause. Then Nina sighed. "Okay. I deserved that. I've been a bitch recently, I know. I've been getting super focused on work and taking it out on you. I'm sorry. Okay?"

It felt so good to hear her say it, to know that Nina had also recognized the growing issues between them. To say they'd cleared the air might have gone a bit far, but Keira felt like something had changed between them, even if it was just the sensation of unspoken irritation being lifted from her shoulders. It wasn't always easy to have difficult conversations, but Milo was right about keeping things aboveboard and honest. It did make life easier.

"Can you tell me how you are now?" Nina asked, trying again.

Keira softened a little. "I'm good. Sort of. Actually, no, I'm in a weird place, to be honest."

"What's going on?" Nina asked. "Elliot was whistling this morning, then he spoke to you on the phone and stormed out of the office."

"Oh," Keira said, deflating. "Yeah, I gave him an earful."

"You did?" Rather than irritated, Nina sounded impressed. "Why? What's going on?"

"He keeps changing his mind about what he wants from me," Keira said, venting her frustrations at Nina just like she'd once done in the past. "It's driving me crazy. And I can't get my own thoughts in order because I'm always instinctively trying to please him." There was a long silence. "Nina?"

"Sorry, I just got an email in from Elliot. He said he's changing the cover of the last magazine? Ditching the Paris one. What the hell is he thinking? It's already in circulation!"

Keira's stomach twisted. "I think that might be my fault. I kinda shouted at him about it. It's everywhere I go. It's like it's haunting me."

"Well, I guess that goes some way to show you how much he values you here," Nina said. "Because changing the cover is going to lose him a ton of money."

Keira could hardly believe it. Never in a million years did she think he would actually pull the cover on her behalf. But the fact he would, for her, made her feel infinitely better about everything. It felt like, for the first time, her company was actually looking out for her rather than just exploiting her love life.

"Hey, Nina, can I ask some advice?" Keira asked.

"Sure. Fire away."

"I've met a guy. He's funny, smart, and so, so handsome. But I don't whether I should pursue it."

"Do it," Nina said without missing a beat. "Wanna know why I've been such a bitch recently? Well, the guy who proposed to me when I was younger, the guy I turned down, the love of my life, he just got married. He's only person I've ever really loved and I turned him down for my job, for meaningless encounters. So if you want my very jaded advice, then you should grab hold of any and every opportunity in life you can."

Keira felt terrible for Nina. She had always viewed her as so fearless and put together. It surprised her to know she was harboring secret heartache.

"But what if it's just a rebound?" she asked timidly. "What if I end up hurt again?"

She thought of Bryn's couch, of the evenings she'd spent watching TV and eating junk food. She never wanted to go back to that place of inertia again. She didn't even want to take the risk of her heart breaking.

"You can't be scared of that," Nina said. "You can't let the possibility of heartbreak stop you from taking a chance."

Keira nodded, listening to Nina's advice intently. There was still a suspicion lingering in her mind that Nina was talking on behalf of the company, rather than for Keira's sake, but either way, she was right.

"Thanks, Nina," she said.

She ended the call, knowing exactly what she needed to do.

CHAPTER TWENTY FOUR

Keira was surprised by how calm she felt now that she'd finally made the decision to call Milo. She thought her hands would be shaking, or her heart beating faster, but she was calm in her decisiveness.

She listened to the sound of ringing on the other end. It kept ringing and ringing. Finally, the call cut to voicemail. Milo hadn't answered.

Keira ended the call and put her cell phone down, looking at it ponderously. She wondered if Milo was deliberately avoiding her. It didn't seem likely, considering what she knew of him. He didn't seem like the avoiding type. He'd be far more likely to answer the call and tell her outright he didn't want to speak to her than to just ignore her. She wondered if perhaps he was at work.

Either way, he would see he'd missed a call from her at some point, and she was confident that once he did he'd get in touch to let her know how he felt either way.

With nothing left to do but wait, Keira decided to spend the rest of the day getting the final few Christmas presents for Shelby and David, Felix, Maxine, and Nina, who'd made it back onto her Christmas gift list following their reconciliation.

She headed toward the busy shopping center of Stockholm, going in and out of stores, selecting appropriate gifts for her nearest and dearest. Then her stomach grumbled and she realized she hadn't eaten yet today. She stopped in a trendy cafe and ordered a salad.

As she was eating, Keira looked around at the people in the cafe. There was a woman, Bryn's age she guessed, breastfeeding her baby at her table. She looked so confident, unashamed to be feeding her child in public, and Keira wondered whether she'd be a good candidate for an interview. She waited until she'd placed the child into its stroller before approaching.

"I'm a writer," she explained after introducing herself. She was getting used to this pitch now, of interrupting people and asking to speak to them. It had become almost second nature. "Do you mind if I speak to you?"

"Not at all!" the woman said. "I'd love it. I don't get anywhere near enough adult conversation these days. There's only so much baby talk one can make without going a bit crazy." She gestured to her baby, sleeping contentedly in its stroller.

Keira took a seat. "You're taking charge of the childcare? Is your partner working?"

"Yes, it made sense. I know, it seems *so* patriarchal." She rolled her eyes. "But I wanted to be with my baby at home. It'll only be for a year, and it's not an experience I want to forgo."

Keira nodded. She started writing down the young mother's words. "And may I ask if you and your partner are married?"

"You may," the woman said, laughing. "We're not. And we don't plan on it. We live together, and we planned to have a child, but we have no intention of marrying."

"I'm learning that this is quite a common setup in Sweden," Keira said.

"It's very common in Scandinavia. Honestly, I find it strange other countries find it strange, that other cultures don't do the same. What does marriage achieve? What's it for? Just some paper and legal stuff. It doesn't change anything."

"I think people want security," Keira said, feeling the need to defend her own culture, or at least, a position she'd previously held, before having her belief system shaken. She laughed then. "And a party."

"Parties, yes," the woman said. "But we throw them all the time, for all kinds of other things, so there's not enough impetus there to marry. Security, well, that's another matter. I for one would not want to be in a relationship where I felt that the other person was only with me because we signed a piece of paper a few years ago. If my partner doesn't love me anymore, I'd prefer he leave. I have a right to be in a relationship with someone who adores me, not someone who's just there because of a sense of obligation."

"What about your baby, though?" Keira asked. Though she understood the woman's position, part of her couldn't help but feel it was a little selfish. Her own father had left, not paying heed to his obligation, and she'd had a myriad of difficulties in her life since. She couldn't fully get behind such a self-centered way of being.

"There are some things I won't be able to protect her from. The best I can do is be happy, work on myself, and show her what resilience is. She deserves that in her mother."

Keira thought of her own mom, the long-suffering Mallory, who used guilt to get her own way, who always seemed to be harboring some kind of resentment, who had a tendency to slip into melodrama. Her dad leaving had been awful, yes, but Mallory's martyrdom attitude had certainly made it worse. She recalled

Heidi's and Ulrich's words, about no one appreciating a martyr. They were so right.

"I wonder though," Keira said, focusing back on the woman, "whether the symbolic gesture of marriage is important to relationships? And to a child's sense of well-being?"

The woman shrugged. "Maybe in a culture where it's considered weird not to. But most kids are born out of wedlock here. It's not unusual or frowned upon. So they feel just as secure as the next kid. My parents were married and it never bothered me."

Keira nodded, writing down the woman's words. She wasn't sure how much she agreed with the young mother, but her comments had certainly given her food for thought. She had always dreamed of marrying one day. It had always been at the back of her mind, just like it had for Shelby and Maxine. But why? Because that's what people did? Because she believed marriage *meant* something specific when it actually didn't mean much at all? She mulled the thoughts over and over in her mind.

*

Keira didn't hear from Milo for the rest of the day. She decided to head back to the B&B, bringing some takeout sushi back with her. Just as she was settling down to eat, her phone rang. It was Milo.

Keira's heart leapt into her throat. She answered the call.

"I've been working all day," he began. "I'm glad you called. How are you?"

"Me?" Keira replied. "Well, my mind is less scrambled than it was yesterday morning, that's for sure." She took a deep breath, taking a leaf out of Milo's book of honesty. "So I was calling to tell you I really like you."

He laughed. "Good. I like you too."

"You do?" she replied. "I wasn't sure if I'd offended you. You didn't try to get in touch."

"I was giving you space," he said. "I made it clear where my intentions lay. It was you who needed to work out how you felt. So I respected your need for space to do that."

Keira couldn't help but burst out laughing. It was so crazy how much those mind games were so ingrained in her head that even with someone as upfront as Milo she'd been agonizing over whether he really liked her or not.

"So, just to clarify, you're into me?" she asked, giggling.

"Oh yes, big time," Milo said. "I've never met someone like you. It's been very difficult not seeing you. I wanted to call you very badly."

Keira was so relieved. It was also so thrilling and exciting to know he liked her so much.

"Shall we meet tomorrow?" she asked.

"I'd like that," he replied. "And you do mean for a date, right?"

"Yes," Keira replied, laughing. "You can show me more of Stockholm."

"I'll pick you up from your hotel and take you to breakfast. How about that?"

"That sounds perfect," Keira replied. She was about to finish the call when she remembered the situation with Elliot, with him being in possession of what were supposed to be private diary entries. Milo needed to know. "I have to tell you something."

"Oh?" he asked.

"It has to do with my article." Keira bit her lip, anxious to break the news. "I wrote about you. I wasn't going to include the passage without your consent but I accidentally sent it to my boss. And, well, he loves it. Now I don't know what to do."

"I don't mind," Milo said, before she'd even finished her sentence.

"You don't?" she asked, surprised. "You don't mind people reading about some of our intimate moments?"

"Well, how intimate did it get? I mean, you didn't mention *that*, did you?" he asked.

Keira barked out a laugh. "NO! It's romance, Milo, not erotica."

He laughed too. "Then I don't mind at all. If anything, it's exciting. I've never had a woman write about me. It's quite romantic."

Keira felt a smile spread across her lips. She should've known he'd be cool with it, that he'd see it through the rose-tinted glasses rather than feel betrayed, or as though she were profiting from him. Still, she was ambivalent. Even with Milo's consent, she still wasn't completely certain that she wanted this particular aspect of her life out there. But then she realized she was probably just being contrary because she was annoyed with Elliot!

They finished making arrangements and then ended the call. Keira had a warm feeling in her stomach, a sense of peace, like everything was finally right in the world.

She tucked into her sushi and wrote up her notes from the day. Then, that night as she slept, she dreamed again of her flowing

143

white gown, the snow, and Milo, her perfect groomsman, waiting for her at the end of the aisle.

CHAPTER TWENTY FIVE

True to his word, Milo was waiting outside Keira's B&B bright and early the next morning, his backside leaning against his little blue car, two takeaway coffees in his hands.

A grin burst across Keira's lips as she hurried toward him.

"For me?" she asked, as he held out one of the cups.

Milo nodded. Keira planted a kiss on his cheek. It felt like the most natural thing in the world.

"Why do I feel like you have something extravagant planned for the day?" she asked, looking at the car. "Have you planned a day trip?"

"There's a castle I really want to see. It's a bit of a drive, though. It's a few hours outside of Stockholm."

Keira sipped her coffee. "I love castles. And I don't mind road trips."

"Great. I packed some stuff for breakfast, in case you hadn't had any."

"I haven't," Keira told him. Milo had thought of everything. He was so considerate.

She got in the passenger side of his car and looked in the back seat, where there was a wicker basket filled with goodies. She noticed a tube of caviar paste and, grimacing, pulled it out and waved it at him. "What is this?"

"It's a delicacy," he replied, laughing.

"Squeezy caviar?" Keira replied, dissolving into giggles.

Milo started the car and then pulled away from the hotel. They were heading southeast, Keira noted.

"This is exciting," she said. "I haven't Stockholm properly yet. It will be nice to see more of Sweden. And since I have you trapped in a car for a few hours, I can ask you all kinds of probing questions."

He shrugged. "Fire away. There's no question off limits as far as I'm concerned."

Keira decided to put that to the test. "Okay. Tell me all about your last relationship, then. I've told you my romantic history, now it's your turn."

145

"Sure," Milo replied. She may as well have asked him what his favorite ice cream flavor was. He didn't seem fazed in the slightest. "Her name was Tindra. We were together for five years."

"Five years!" Keira exclaimed. "That's a long time. What happened?"

"She cheated on me," Milo told her. It was the first time she'd heard him sound anything less than happy.

"I'm so sorry."

"It was devastating," Milo said. "I was so, so sad. I've not dated much since then. And I've not had a serious relationship since."

Keira didn't know what to say. She felt bad for probing now and fell into silence, sipping her coffee while watching the world go by.

"My longest relationship has been two years," she said. "I'm twenty-eight. That's pretty bad, isn't it?"

"Bad?" Milo asked, looking curious. "Why would it be bad?"

She shrugged. "Because it shows I'm not very good at keeping relationships alive."

"Who cares?" Milo said. "Who are you trying to prove yourself to?"

Keira pondered his question. She wasn't sure what the answer was, but even before she'd become a writer with an audience, she always felt watched and judged by some imagined force. Two years with Zachary had seemed like something she'd needed to do to prove that she could, that she wasn't as damaged by her absent father as crazy Bryn was, or her perpetually lonely mom, for that matter. If someone could stay with her for two whole years, she couldn't be too much of a lost cause, could she? But honestly, who was she trying to impress? Why did it matter anyway?

"Let's change the conversation," Keira said. "I'm hungry. Shall I make up some sandwiches?"

"Please," Milo said.

"You want squeezy caviar in yours?" Keira joked.

"Of course," Milo replied, completely seriously. "And cheese and olives."

Keira leaned into the back, selecting all the foodstuffs. She made up their sandwiches, and Milo turned on the radio, singing along loudly to a Swedish pop song she didn't know. Keira looked over at him and smiled. This was exactly where she needed to be.

*

Kalmar Castle was absolutely wonderful. It was built in a Baroque style, and all the staff were dressed as if from the middle ages. Not only were the green areas around the castle beautiful, but there were bunny rabbits hopping around freely! There was a cemetery nearby filled with interesting and unique headstones, and of course, Milo was having the time of his life, walking around the ramparts and sitting on the cannons. Keira herself was more taken with the furnishings inside the castle, which were extravagantly gorgeous. She and Milo spent at least two hours on the site, either inside the castle or wandering its courtyards and lawns, but the time flew by, as it always did, Keira noted, when she spent it with Milo.

"We'd better head back," Milo said, looking at his watch. "I've made a reservation at a restaurant in Stockholm."

Keira was a little sad to leave the castle behind. It had been a lovely place to spend the day, and she was looking forward to immortalizing it in her article. She remembered then about the passage she'd sent to Elliot accidentally about Milo. She had no plans to use it, but she wondered how Milo himself would actually feel about being in her article.

"You know my article…" she began. "The one I'm writing about Sweden?"

"Yes?" he said, looking over at her from the steering wheel.

"Are you sure you wouldn't mind if I included you in it? I don't have to use your name if you don't want me to."

"I wouldn't mind at all," Milo told her. "Actually, I'd quite like it. If you're going to disappear out of my life in a few days' time, it would be nice to have something to remember you by."

Keira felt her stomach drop. She hadn't given any thought to what would happen in the future. In fact, leaving Sweden hadn't been on her mind at all. But it seemed as if Milo had already thought about it, and was already prepared for her to go away and never return. Maybe that was why he was so open, so forthright, because he knew there was no future in it.

"Have I said something wrong?" Milo asked.

Keira shook her head. "No. Just… I don't like thinking about endings. That's all."

They fell silent. Not even Swedish pop songs could lighten the mood.

Keira spent the rest of the journey processing her feelings. When they reached the outskirts of Stockholm, Milo spoke for the first time in a long time.

"Would you prefer me to drop you back at the hotel?" he asked. "I feel as if you would like some space from me."

Keira shook her head. "No. I want to spend as much time with you as I can."

She snapped her lips shut. Milo might be used to brutal honesty, but Keira wasn't. Had she revealed too much?

"That's fine by me," he said, and he continued on to the restaurant.

After parking, Milo and Keira went inside the restaurant. It had a very pleasant atmosphere, with large windows filled with plants. Just like the last place he'd taken her, there was nothing pretentious about this place. It seemed down to earth, with most tables occupied with groups of friends rather than couples on dates.

Keira took a seat and looked over the menu. The entrees on offer included meatballs (of course), a herring platter, steak, and sea bass fillet, but Keira's gaze was drawn to something even more unique; the reindeer burger.

"Reindeer?" she said, looking over her menu at Milo. "Like, actual reindeer?"

He nodded. "Rudolph."

She began to laugh. "I don't know if I could eat Rudolph!"

But part of coming abroad was experiencing new cultures, and that meant being brave when it came to food. She'd already chickened out of trying Milo's strange savory cake and squeezy caviar. Now was time to be brave.

"I'm going to do it," she said. "I'm going to order the reindeer."

Milo looked amused.

When the food arrived, Keira felt nervous to try it. But she finally bit the bullet and was pleasantly surprised. Reindeer tasted pretty delicious.

After getting over the nerves of her meal, Keira relaxed into the rest of the evening. She let Milo's comments earlier sift out of her mind.

They finished eating and the server came over with the bill.

"I'll get this," Milo said.

"Are you sure?" Keira replied. "I know it's not how things are usually done. Don't feel like you have to pay just because I'm an American girl who expects it!"

"But you are," he laughed. "And I don't mind, I want to treat you."

Keira smiled and allowed him to pay for her meal, making a mental note that next time—if there was a next time—she'd foot the bill, to keep things equitable as he, a Swedish boy, would expect.

They both stood, collecting their things.

"I had one more surprise planned," Milo told her. "But it's been a long day and I understand if you'd like to go home now."

Keira shook her head. "Not at all. What did you have in mind?"

"This way," Milo said, directing her toward the waterfront.

To Keira's surprise, there was a small beach. Milo laid out a blanket for her to sit on.

"It's kind of freezing," Keira said. As romantic as the gesture was, she didn't much feel like freezing to death for the sake of politeness.

But Milo had planned ahead. He took another blanket from his bag and wrapped it around Keira's shoulders. Then, from his bag, he also pulled a thermos flask.

"What's that?" Keira laughed. "And has that been in the car with us all day?"

Milo nodded. "It's hot chocolate. It'll still be warm. If there's one thing us Swedes know how to do, it's keep out the cold!"

They sat, and Milo poured her a cup of chocolate. She took a sip. It was rich and creamy. And yes, still warm. Then Milo pointed up at the sky.

"This is why I wanted to bring you here tonight," he said. "It's a clear evening and the forecast said we'd be able to see them."

Keira frowned and looked up, then realized that the Northern Lights were shining above her. It was breathtaking. She couldn't believe something so beautiful could exist. She turned to face Milo, overwhelmed with emotion. But to her disbelief, he was no longer looking at the Northern Lights at all. In fact, he was texting!

"Milo?" she said, shocked that he wasn't sharing the beautiful moment with her.

"Sorry," he said, putting his phone down. "My friend just invited me to a bar. I was just telling him I'd be free in a couple of hours. Is that okay?"

Keira felt herself deflate. Was Milo ditching her?

"I thought we were on a date," she said.

"We are. Now. But after?"

She frowned, confused. "Well, the date doesn't just end like that, does it? I thought that maybe you'd come back to my room."

"I still can," he said, looking confused. "After the bar."

Keira couldn't help but feel furious with him. There was nothing romantic about him ditching her for a few hours so he could see his friends at a bar! She felt reality come crashing down, dragging her down from cloud nine with a bump.

"What's wrong, Keira?" Milo asked. "You've gone quiet on me again."

149

"You've ruined our date," she snapped. "Everything was perfect. But now I just feel like you want to see your friends." She folded her arms. She sounded so petulant and hated herself for throwing a tantrum.

"I won't go," he said. "I'm sorry. I didn't realize you'd mind. I didn't know it would upset you."

She folded her arms and looked away. On what planet would someone *not* mind their date leaving them to go to a bar?

Milo took her hands. "I can see them anytime, but I have a time limit with you. I'll text him now and say I'm too busy."

Keira felt bad. And for some reason, Milo's reasonableness was only making her feel worse. It was as though she were some overemotional child and he the calm, rational parent.

"There," Milo said. "I've texted him to say no. Do you want more chocolate?"

"No," Keira mumbled. "I think I want to go back to the hotel."

"Oh. Okay," Milo said. He seemed utterly perplexed over why things had gone so wrong with her. "Am I coming too?" he asked.

Keira didn't know what to say. He'd cancelled his plans for her but she didn't feel able to put aside her sadness over his mistake in making them in the first place.

"Yeah, of course," she said finally. "But I'm super tired from the day."

She hoped her intention was clear. But Milo, being Milo, still had to get absolute certain clarification.

"Is that your way of saying no sex tonight?"

Keira felt her cheeks burn. "Yes. That's what I'm saying."

"Got it," he said.

But Keira really wasn't sure he did.

CHAPTER TWENTY SIX

Keira lay in bed staring at the ceiling, listening to the sound of Milo snoring. He'd woken her for what must have been the tenth time that night. She groaned, rolling over and pressing a pillow over her ears. Then she saw the clock beside the bed. It was six a.m. She'd have to wake up soon and it didn't feel like she'd even slept!

She tried to calm her frustrated mind, to take some deep breaths and fall back to sleep. But Milo let out another loud snore. Unable to hold back her irritation, Keira grabbed her pillow and threw it at him. It bounced off his face onto the floor.

Milo's eyes pinged open. "Is it morning?"

Keira didn't feel like speaking to him. She was still feeling wounded about the argument last night. She rolled away from him.

"Not yet."

"Why are you awake then?" Milo asked, never one to mince words.

"Because you're snoring obnoxiously loudly," Keira replied, tersely.

Milo laughed. "Oh no. It's my deviated septum. I'm sorry. There's not a lot I can do about it, though."

Keira just grunted in response.

She heard Milo shuffling, and felt his arms loop around her from behind. "You're angry," he said. "And I don't think it's just because of my snoring."

Keira sighed and squeezed her eyes shut.

"Hmmm," she heard Milo say in her ear. "Am I supposed to guess? Like a game?"

"No," Keira said. "You're supposed to be quiet and let me get at least five minutes of sleep."

"What if I were to fetch us some coffee and breakfast?" Milo suggested. "So that when you wake up it's all there for you?"

Keira sat up abruptly, shoving his arms off her. "Fine. I'm never going to get back to sleep, am I?" She reached for the remote and turned on the TV.

Milo pulled himself up to sitting beside her. But he didn't look worried about her little outburst. If anything, he seemed amused. It annoyed Keira even further. Surely he could appreciate why she

151

was still frosty with him, after how he'd ruined their date by asking to ditch her.

"This show is in Swedish," Milo commented.

"So?" Keira said, folding her arms. "I can work out the gist of what's happening."

She couldn't, of course, but she wanted to save face.

"Hmmm," Milo said again. Then he got out of bed. "The kitchen will be open and serving breakfast. I'm going to go and fetch us both something. When I get back, how about you tell me why you're really mad at me? Because it can't just be my deviated septum that is making you so cross."

He walked over to the door where the complimentary bathrobe was hanging and slipped it on.

"You can't go like that!" Keira exclaimed.

Milo didn't seem fazed at all. He just shrugged. "It's fine. I'm sure they've seen it all before."

Keira watched, mortified, as Milo left the room in nothing but a fluffy bathrobe.

Without him, the room felt suddenly very empty. Keira shut off the TV and its incessant Swedish buzz. She wallowed in her tired grumpiness for a moment, then realized that Milo was going to be too stubborn to just apologize about last night, because he wanted her to articulate herself to him honestly and truthfully. She sighed, infuriated by the logic of it all. She'd never learned how to have calm conversations without them turning into arguments and petty insults. She wondered if Milo had ever lost his temper in his life.

Her opportunity to fall back asleep well and truly gone, she got up and showered. But as soon as she was clean and dried, she climbed back to bed, too tired and grumpy to choose an outfit or put her makeup on.

A moment later, the door opened, and Milo walked in with a tray in his hands. It was filled to the brim with buffet foods. There was an entire pot of steaming coffee. Keira flushed with embarrassment.

"Did you really walk into the dining room and fill up a tray with food?" she asked with exasperation.

"Yes," Milo said simply.

He came in and placed it on the bed. Amongst the breads and cheeses were cold cuts of meat, berries, jam, soured milk, and an entire tube of squeezy caviar.

"Milo!" she cried, and this time she couldn't help but start to laugh. "You took the whole tube?"

"I'm quite sure none of the tourists will mind," he said, smirking.

Keira sighed. She took the coffee he poured for her and buttered herself a hunk of bread, laying a few slices of smoked ham on top of it.

"Thank you," she muttered as she bit into her food.

"You're welcome," Milo said, the smirk still on his lips. "What happened to our telly show?"

"I had a shower and turned it off to save electricity," she said, lying again to save face.

"Ah," he said, knowingly. "I thought you looked less grubby."

"Milo!" she cried again, and he dissolved into laughter.

"I'm sorry," he said. "You're just very cute when you're mad. And very easy to wind up. So, are you ready to tell me why you threw a pillow at me this morning?"

"Because you kept me awake with your snoring," she implored.

"And..." he pressed.

"And because I'm still mad at you about last night!"

Milo nodded. "There. That wasn't too hard, was it?"

Keira put her bread down and frowned at him. "You're infuriating, do you know that? Why can't you just say sorry?"

"I thought I already did."

"That was last night."

"It requires two apologies?"

"YES! It requires as many apologies as it takes until I stop being mad!"

"Got it," Milo said with a nod. "I'm sorry, Keira. I'm sorry. Keira, I am truly sorry."

"Oh, shut up!" Keira said, hitting him with another pillow.

Milo laughed. But then, once he'd recovered, he grew serious. "Keira, I actually am sorry that I upset you. It hadn't occurred to me that making arrangements with my friends would upset you. But I can see now why it was insensitive."

Keira pursed her lips.

"Am I getting closer?" he asked.

"Maybe..." Keira said.

"And I really like you," he added. "I don't want to screw it up. Especially over something like that. So easily avoided. I have learned my lesson. I will speak to you first before making plans."

Keira nodded. She could tell his apology was heartfelt and that he truly understood why she'd reacted how she had.

"Okay," she said. "You're forgiven."

"I am?" he asked. "Phew!" He blew air out his mouth. "I wasn't sure if we'd make it through our first fight."

"It wasn't a fight," she said, rolling her eyes.

"Yeah, I think it was," he replied. "People don't throw pillows for no reason."

"Sorry about that," Keira said, blushing.

"Don't be," he told her. "I always want to know when you're mad. Or else how can I change things? That said, there is literally nothing I can do about the snoring. You'll have to get used to it."

Keira laughed. She picked her bread up and began to eat again. With the air cleared, she felt much better. And she realized then that relationships—romantic or otherwise—were always going to go through little bumps of miscommunication and misunderstanding. It was how they were dealt with that mattered. And Milo had dealt with that one perfectly, really. He had not made her feel bad about her feelings, or the childish way she'd expressed them, nor had he turned it into a fight or reacted defensively. He'd just been very Milo about the whole thing. He'd been, well, perfect.

"I have a question," Keira said then.

Milo looked over at her, eyebrows raised. "Fire away."

"Well, it's more of a request actually," she said.

"I'm listening."

"You know how I was so mad at you last night, I said no sex…"

"Yes?"

"Well, I'm not mad anymore."

A grin spread across Milo's lips. "Say no more."

*

A whole morning disappeared before their very eyes. When midday arrived, neither wanted yet to leave the bed, so Milo went to a corner shop nearby and picked up sandwiches, which they ate in bed before resuming their marathon lovemaking. When the sky started to darken, Keira flopped back against the bed, exhausted.

"I'm done," she announced. "My legs are jelly. I can't focus straight. We have to stop."

She looked over at Milo, giggling. He propped himself up on his elbows and smiled at her, his eyes sparkling with desire.

"You are very beautiful," he said, his fingers playing with her hair.

"So are you."

"I really like you," he added.

154

"I really like you too."

Milo continued. "I like you so much I want to take you home to meet my parents."

Keira's eyes widened. "You do?"

Milo nodded. "Yes. I want them to get to know you. And you them. But is that too much? I understand if you feel like it is too soon."

Keira lay back against the pillow, still trying to catch her breath. She mulled over Milo's proposition. All the different pieces of advice she'd been given over the last few days began swirling in her mind. But above all else, she remembered Bryn telling her not to overthink things, to trust her instincts. And her instincts were telling her to go for it, to be brave, to experience everything she could with this man while she had the chance and throw caution to the wind.

She looked back at Milo. "Yes."

"Yes?"

"Yes. I'd like to meet them too."

He looked thrilled. "I'll call my mom right now."

"NO!" Keira cried. "Not from the bed we've just been, you know. Go and do it over there." She pointed at the desk.

Milo laughed. "You're strange." But he did as she said.

Keira watched him, gazing adoringly upon his body. He really was a unique soul, a one in a million guy. She felt lucky, no, blessed, that their paths had crossed. It felt a bit like fate.

And if she really took Bryn's advice and listened to her gut instinct, then she would go as far as to say she was falling for him.

She was falling in love.

CHAPTER TWENTY SEVEN

Keira woke up in Milo's strong arms the next morning, feeling content and warm. But it didn't take long for the calm feeling to fade when she remembered that yesterday she'd agreed to meet his family. She was struck with sudden nerves and sat up, pushing him off.

Milo stirred beside her. "Morning. Did my deviated septum keep you awake at all last night?"

He was murmuring, still half asleep, but Keira had much more important things on her mind than Milo's snoring.

"What time are we seeing your family?" she blurted, ignoring his question.

"I told Mom we'd head over after breakfast," he said with a yawn.

Keira bolted right out of bed. "I have to get ready," she said. "What should I wear?"

As she began flapping around the room in panic, Milo started to come to his senses, and he looked at her curiously before starting to laugh.

"What on earth are you doing?" he asked, sitting up fully and watching her with an amused frown.

"I'm trying to get ready," she said. "But I can't find my black jeans!" She crouched down, sifting through the open suitcase at the foot of her bed and throwing items haphazardly around her.

"Calm down," she heard Milo say from somewhere above her, out of view. "They're not monsters. They don't mind what you wear. Just dress like you normally would."

"So these stone-wash jeans would be appropriate?" she said sarcastically, holding up a pair of—perhaps misjudged on reflection—skinny, ripped, pale blue jeans. Then she stood, another panicked thought overcoming her. "And what about my hair?" she cried, hurrying to the mirror. "Does it look okay? Should I put it up or wear it down loose?"

In the reflection of the mirror, she saw Milo getting out of bed. He came calmly over to her, wrapping his arms around her chest. He pressed a kiss into her cheek.

"They will love you," he reassured her reflection. "I promise you. You have nothing to worry about."

Keira took a deep breath. Behind her, Milo felt so solid and warm. His presence soothed her. In his arms, she began to relax.

She turned to face him, gazing up into his eyes with adoration. How had she found such a sweet man? It seemed like fate was intervening.

"Oh," Keira said then, as her gaze fell past Milo to the strewn clothes on the floor, falling on the pair of black jeans she'd been searching for. "There they are."

He laughed and released her. She scooped the black jeans up off the floor and slid them on. Then she paired them with a simple plaid shirt. She hoped the outfit made her look down to earth but not sloppy. Approachable but not lazy.

"Ta-da," she said, once she was dressed. "How did I do?"

Milo chuckled. "You look beautiful. You always do. Now can we please go and eat? I am starving."

Keira nodded, and together they waded through the discarded clothes and out of the room.

Elsewhere in the hotel, the breakfast buffet was being served, and it filled the halls with the smell of delicious foods. But Keira and Milo didn't feel like B&B food, instead preferring to head out to a cafe. Out on the street, the sky was milky gray, threatening, as it had for days, to snow.

As they strolled the streets toward the cafe, Keira felt Milo's hand reaching for hers. She let him lace his fingers through hers, smiling to herself at the sensation of their first handhold. It felt so right, so natural. And his hands helped keep out the biting cold.

Once in the cafe, Keira, who had grown so accustomed to the Swedish-style breakfast now and had decided to completely ditch any pretense of a diet, ordered a large open sandwich and super-strength coffee. But when they sat to eat, Keira found her appetite had diminished. She picked at her food.

"You've hardly eaten," Milo commented. "Are you okay?"

Keira grimaced. "I guess I'm anxious. It's not like me to lose my appetite. Or freak out about what color jeans I'm wearing."

As she said it aloud, it occurred to her that her level of anxiety matched the amount that she wanted Milo's family to like her. And that meant one thing and one thing only. He was important. Her stomach swirled with the realization.

"Is there anything I need to know before I meet your parents?" she asked, that familiar sensation of panic arising again.

"Like what?" Milo asked, smiling as he shook his head. "You mean like whether they have purple skin and three eyes?"

Keira rolled her eyes. "No. I don't mean that. I mean, like, are there any topics I shouldn't bring up? Politics, for example? Or, I don't know, which basketball player is better?"

Milo chuckled again. He rubbed her arm. "I promise you, my parents are both completely normal people who you can ask completely normal questions to. They both love debating politics so you won't offend them in that regard, and everyone knows it's LeBron James, so there's nothing controversial there." He winked. Keira couldn't help but smile. But Milo continued speaking, poking his sandwich as he did so. "That said, that's just my parents. Regina, on the other hand…"

Keira's eyes widened. "Your sister? What's wrong with her?"

"Like I said, she's the smartest person in the world," Milo explained. "She'll tell you all about meteorites and star systems and other stuff like that until your ears bleed or you drop dead from boredom. The trick is to be firm. But not too firm. She's been known to bite."

Keira's eyes grew wider still. Then Milo burst out laughing.

"I'm only joking!" he exclaimed. "Honestly, you should have seen your face."

Keira scowled at him. "Not funny, Milo. I want this to go well."

"It will," he reassured her, reaching across the table and squeezing her arm. "Regina is a normal person. My parents are normal people. They will love you. There's no way they can't."

Keira looked into his eyes and knew he was speaking from the heart.

*

After breakfast, they hailed a cab to take them to the small town where Milo's parents lived. It was a few towns over from Stockholm, not far, but the drive sent them crisscrossing up into the mountains. It was truly beautiful and Keira marveled at the view.

"The mountains are incredible," she said, gazing up through the window at them.

"I know," Milo said. "I was very lucky to have them to look at as a child."

She remembered her strange question from before when she'd first met Milo and he reminded her of Jossi, about whether he'd climbed a mountain.

"You were never tempted to climb them?" she asked him now, amused at how the topic had come full circle.

"Nope," he said. "Dad and I would hike in the countryside, but nothing as extreme as mountaineering."

"Kind of tempting though," she said, looking up to their snowy peaks. "The view from there must be incredible. Imagine seeing the Northern Lights from the top of that mountain."

"I guess so," he said, smiling.

Keira was so entranced by the mountains that she was shocked when the cab pulled to a halt.

"We're here?" she asked, surprised.

Milo nodded. "Yes. The house is right there."

Keira peered out the window and saw a gorgeous little house, right on the edge of the mountain. It had a sweeping pathway leading to the front porch.

"But it practically is in the mountains!" Keira commented.

Milo laughed. "Yes. I thought it was very funny how you were talking about climbing them when really I grew up in them! And yes, the Northern Lights are spectacular from here. If the sky is clear tonight, we can stay up and look at them."

"No wonder your sister became an astrophysicist," Keira murmured, awed by the wonder of it all.

Just then, the porch door opened, and a woman hurried out toward the cab. She was short, rather plump, and had dark, curly hair. Her grin was unmistakably Milo's. This, Keira realized, must be his mother. And she looked overjoyed to have her son home.

Milo opened the back door and left the cab, heading straight into his mother's open arms. Keira took a deep breath and got out of the cab, too.

"You must be Keira!" Milo's mother exclaimed, turning her attention from her son to Keira. "I'm Yolanta. Oh, it's so wonderful to meet you." She reached out and took Keira's had, pumping it up and down enthusiastically. Then she pulled her into her bosom, hugging her tightly.

Keira felt herself instantly relax. Milo's mother was clearly an extremely personable woman, and very loving. Keira felt immediately at ease in her company.

"I can't wait to sit down and learn all about you," Yolanta added. "Come in, come in. Do you like coffee?"

"I love it," Keira said.

She followed Milo and his mother inside the house. It was very warm inside, a homely cottage with walls painted a rich, burnt orange color. There were tons of potted plants all over the place, too, making the entrance hall feel a bit like a jungle, or some kind of Moroccan palace.

"You have a lovely home," Keira commented.

"Thank you, darling," Yolanta said. "This way. Let me introduce you to Nils."

They went into the living room. It was a compact room, taken up mainly by a huge, squishy couch. Sitting on it was a thin gentleman who had Milo's eyes, and a woman who Keira assumed to be Regina, the astrophysicist sister. They both stood as she entered.

"Keira," Nils said first. He opened his arms to her. Keira hesitated before moving into them for an embrace. He was very wiry, a tall, bony man. It wasn't often she hugged older men, having no father of her own, and the sensation was unfamiliar. "We've heard a lot about you." He moved away and gestured to Regina. "This is our daughter."

"Hi," Keira said, shyly, waving at Regina.

But Regina opened her arms too, pulling Keira into them like some kind of mother hen. Keira's instinct was always to recoil from overt displays of affection, but she knew that was more her problem than anyone else's, and let the hug happen.

"I'm just making some coffee," Yolanta said.

"I'll do it, darling," Nils replied. He stood and headed for the door, embracing Milo on his way out of the room.

"Please sit," Yolanta said to Keira.

She took one of the seats, glancing about her nervously at the homely furnishings and the myriad family photos plastering the walls. Milo's family was clearly very close and loving. She couldn't help but compare it to her own family, who, though loving, weren't always particularly close.

It didn't take long for Keira to relax into the company of Milo's family. And soon, she realized that this was somewhere she could really see herself fitting in.

*

Dinner was a loud, jolly affair. Instead of leaving Yolanta to do the work, the whole family cooked together. And they attempted to rope Keira in too.

"But I'm a terrible cook," she protested, blushing.

"Well, now is the time to learn," Regina said. "I'll show you how to prepare the fish."

Keira grimaced. For a novice chef, gutting a fish was really throwing her in at the deep end! But Regina was patient, good at explaining what to do, and Keira found her worries disappear. Soon, she was actually enjoying herself, being part of the bustling dinner-making experience.

She helped Milo set the table.

"Are you coping?" he asked her.

"I am," she said, grinning now. "I'm having a really great time. They're all so lovely."

"I told you," he said.

Regina came in with a salad bowl and placed it on the table. Yolanta followed with wine and glasses. Nils came last with the main fish dish, and he laid it in the middle.

"Grub's up!" he exclaimed.

Everyone sat and began chatting easily. Keira found them so laid back, and she quickly learned where Milo had got his wit from. Everyone! They were so funny. It occurred to Keira that she didn't feel even an ounce of loneliness anymore.

"Keira, you're most welcome to stay for the rest of your trip," Yolanta said. "Staying in hotels all the time must be very tiresome. Don't you miss home?"

"I do," Keira said, surprised.

But her mind was still processing the offer to stay with them. There wasn't much more authentic for her article than being with an actual Swedish family. But more than that, she really liked them and wanted to spend time with them.

"So?" Yolanta asked again. "We'd love to have you here. You're most welcome."

Keira grinned, suddenly confident in her decision. "Actually, that would be wonderful." But she remembered then that all her stuff was in the hotel, the vast majority strewn across the floor.

As if reading her mind, Milo said, "We can head back to the hotel after dinner and collect your things. Check you out. Is that okay?"

"Yes," she said, smiling wide. "It's perfect."

*

Late that night, Keira and Milo sat on the deck at the edge of the mountain. Everyone else had gone to bed, leaving them some privacy, and a bottle of champagne sat bubbling beside them. The view of the water was spectacular. On such a clear evening, she could see all the boats in the harbor.

161

"A toast," Milo said, holding up his glass. "To new beginnings."

As Keira clinked her glass against his, she thought about how just a week ago she'd toasted alone, on the deck of her ship, to her independence, to freedom from relationships. Yet here she was toasting to a new relationship. All at once, all the lessons she'd learned on love during her trip in Sweden converged in her mind, forming one clear picture. She laughed aloud.

"What is it?" Milo asked, looking at her with interest.

"I just realized something," she said, looking him in the eye. "That falling in love doesn't have to mean you lose independence. That you just need to find someone who respects your needs."

"Is that your way of saying you're falling in love with me?" Milo asked.

Keira looked deeply into his eyes. With the stars twinkling in the black sky behind him, he looked extremely beautiful.

"Yes," she said, boldly. "I am."

"Good," he replied. "Because I am too."

CHAPTER TWENTY EIGHT

With Milo snoring softly beside her in bed, Keira typed on her laptop. She had a newfound sense of mental clarity, one that had eluded her the whole trip. Suddenly, everything made perfect sense. She typed the final line of her article and sent it to Elliot. Then she folded her laptop down, content, accomplished, and, more importantly, in love.

*

Breakfast at the Nilsson household was as jolly an affair as dinner. Milo's alarm woke them early, and he led Keira to the kitchen, where his family was already awake. The smell of coffee perfumed the air, and a whole spread of foods had been laid out on the table. It was more elaborate than the cafe breakfasts they'd been eating so far.

"Help yourself," Regina said, handing a mug of steaming coffee to Keira.

Keira filled her plate with bread, cheese, and meats, then settled at the table with the others. All hints of awkwardness she'd felt before had completely melted away. She felt like one of them, like she was at home.

"Keira, I was wondering," Nils said, pausing between huge mouthfuls of food. "Have you ever been ice fishing?"

"No," she replied. "I've never been normal fishing, either. It sounds interesting. What does it involve?"

She remembered the adventurous man Milo had painted of his father and presumed it would be something rather elaborate. His explanation did not disappoint.

"First, we trek to the lake," he said, his eyes sparkling. "Then we drill a hole into the ice and set the bait."

"Then we freeze our asses off sitting around," Milo concluded.

Everyone laughed.

Regina added, "Actually, Dad makes his infamous hot chocolate to keep us toasty warm."

"It sounds amazing," Keira said. She wanted to have as many authentic experiences as possible during her last few days in Sweden.

Milo looked thrilled. "This is literally my favorite thing to do in the world," he said. "But are you sure you're up for it? There's a lot of waiting around. And it's very cold."

"I'm not going to lie," Keira admitted, "the idea of catching a fish does kind of gross me out. But it sounds really interesting. Not an experience I want to pass up."

"Then it's decided," Milo said, addressing his father. "When shall we go?"

"No time like the present," Nils replied. "If everyone's finished eating."

They nodded, and everyone began to tidy up after themselves. Keira noticed how Nils took over the washing up duties from his wife, kissing her on the cheek as he said, "Let me do that, darling."

She smiled at their display of affection. Their relationship seemed so lovely and tender. Keira wondered if she and Milo could have something like that too, one day. She certainly hoped they could. It looked wonderful.

She headed back up to Milo's room to get ready for the day, realizing she had no idea what would be appropriate to wear ice fishing. She hadn't packed for such an occasion.

A moment later, Milo appeared. He was holding a bright red snowsuit.

"This is my mom's spare one," he said. "You can borrow it."

Keira took the suit from his hands and held it up. "This?" she said. "It's very... red."

She noticed the smirk at the corner of Milo's mouth. "We don't want to lose you out in the snow, Keira," he joked.

Keira pulled the suit on over her clothes and then went to look in the mirror. She both felt and looked absurd. Not that there was anything particularly embarrassing about wearing a snowsuit, but it was several sizes too large, the puffiness making it appear bigger still, and it was practically fluorescent. But then she looked over the shoulder of her reflection to see Milo coming up behind her, wearing an equally bright and puffy suit, not red, but green. For the third time during their short relationship, they looked ridiculous together.

Looking at their reflection, Keira couldn't help but laugh. And she realized with a surge of confidence that she'd shed her usual skin of shame. In Milo's presence, she didn't care how silly she looked, be it in a Viking hat or a neon snowsuit. With Milo by her side, there was no such thing as embarrassment. He turned everything into a fun moment, a shared experience, an opportunity to smile. And smile Keira did.

CHAPTER TWENTY NINE

Keira trudged alongside Nils, Regina, and Milo, who were each carrying various types of equipment. They were making the journey to the frozen lake on foot, and the route took them through forests and snow-covered hillsides. Keira was freezing but she didn't care, because the scenery was so breathtakingly beautiful.

Then finally, the trees parted and Keira saw the enormous frozen lake open up before her, like a sheet of gray glass.

"It's amazing," she mused aloud.

They headed down the banks. Keira was reticent to walk on the ice at first, having been told so many times in her life that frozen water wasn't safe, but the Nilsson clan strolled right out, carefree. They'd done this a million times before, so Keira trusted that they knew what they were doing, and she waddled over to join them in her bright red outfit.

Nils began to cut a hole in the ice with what looked like a comically large corkscrew. He drilled it in by hand, then wound it back out in reverse, leaving a perfectly neat hole. Then it was Regina's turn to use her equipment, which consisted of a wire line and bait. Once she'd set it up, everyone stepped back.

"That's it?" Keira asked.

"That's one," Nils said. "We may as well set up a few. Increase our chances."

They paced around the lake, selecting locations that were suitably far enough from the first, drilling the holes and setting the lines.

"Now we just wait?" Keira asked once everything was set up.

"Yup," Milo said.

He unfolded the lightweight camping chairs he'd been carrying, while Nils took the flask of the promised hot chocolate from his bag. The flask was passed from one person to the next, and each poured a little mug of steaming chocolate to drink.

"Looks like it might snow," Nils said, pointing at the gray sky.

Keira was too cold as it was to think about snow. But Regina shook her head.

"I've been keeping up with the reports," she said. "The sky will clear by nightfall. We're going to have a very interesting evening, meteorologically speaking."

"Will we see the Northern Lights?" Keira asked, growing excited. She had adored the sight of them so far, and wanted to utilize as many opportunities to see them as she could.

"Oh yes," Regina said, nodding. "It will probably be the best display of them all year."

"Awesome," Keira said. She just had to make it until nightfall without freezing her butt off. At least the hot chocolate was helping. And the sun set very early at this time of year, so she was sure she'd make it.

"Let's check the lines," Nils said.

They each went over to their respective hole and tugged on the line. Keira tugged on her line and to her surprise, a huge, glistening trout flopped out of the hole. The sight of it was so surprising, Keira screamed and reeled back.

Everyone turned to her.

"Keira's caught one!" she heard Milo call out.

But her attention was too focused on the fish flapping up and down, flying all over the place. It hit her boots and she squealed again. Then Milo was there, right beside her, chuckling in his usual laid-back way. He grabbed the trout expertly, and its fevered flapping ceased. He held it up to her and Keira calmed down instantly.

"Awesome job, Keira," Nils said, coming up beside her and clapping his hand on her shoulder.

Keira beamed, proud of her accomplishment. And, she realized, she wasn't even the slightest bit embarrassed about freaking out in front of them. She couldn't even feel warmth in her cheeks. These people put her so at ease that she felt no hint of awkwardness. It was the greatest feeling in the world.

*

Before long, everyone had grown too cold to remain out on the lake. They began to collect their things just as the sun started setting.

Keira looked up at the sky and, just as Regina promised, it was clear enough to catch a glimpse of the Northern Lights. Somehow, it was even more beautiful than the last time she saw them. The stars seemed brighter, too, as if she were gazing at every star in the universe. It was a humbling experience. She'd never seen anything more beautiful.

Milo came up beside her and she tore her gaze from the beauty to look upon his face. He smiled at her and wrapped an arm around her shoulders, before looking up at the Northern Lights for himself. But Keira had a new view to look at now; Milo. He was so handsome and kind and funny. His personality made him all the more attractive, not to mention his sense of adventure.

He must have noticed her staring then, because he looked down again, smiling his twinkling smile, gazing deeply into her eyes. As the stars twinkled behind him, Milo leaned in to Keira and planted a sumptuous kiss onto her lips. The world melted away and Keira sunk into him, lost in a moment of pure perfection.

CHAPTER THIRTY

Keira's last day in Sweden dawned. She woke with a sense of trepidation. She didn't want this to be the end of her time here. And she most definitely didn't want it to be the end of her and Milo. But they had not discussed the future. She couldn't even picture what a long-distance relationship with him would look like.

Over breakfast, Milo addressed his mother. "I was thinking that since it's Keira's last day today, it might be nice for us to spend the time together. Just the two of us."

As he spoke, Keira could see that he was upset. Clearly, the future was weighing on his shoulders as much as it was hers.

"Of course," Yolanta said, genially. "You two go out and have fun."

They finished eating, called a cab and, once it pulled up outside, said goodbye to the family.

In the backseat, Keira asked Milo, "So what's the grand plan for today then?"

But Milo seemed very quiet. "Keira, we need to talk about the future."

Keira felt a swirling in her gut. "Yes. We do." She reached out and grabbed his hand. "What do you want to do?"

"Honestly," Milo said, "I want you to move to Sweden." Keira's eyes widened and Milo laughed. "But I know that's not realistic."

Keira shook her head. "It's not that. I actually really like the idea. I could see myself living here."

"You could?" he asked, suddenly hopeful.

"But I can't," she finished.

Milo seemed to deflate like a balloon. "I wouldn't feel comfortable moving to New York City," he said, sadly.

"I know." She squeezed his hand. "You told me when I first met you that you were a homebody. I wouldn't expect you to leave this place, your job, and your family for me."

Milo turned his gaze from his lap to meet Keira's. She'd never seen such sadness in them.

"Then what happens next?" he asked.

He seemed to be bracing himself for an ending. But Keira wasn't ready for that. Not by a long shot. She'd learned too much in Sweden, too much from him, to let go this soon.

"Would it be completely crazy to try this long distance?" she suggested. She chewed her lip in consternation. "I mean the world is so much more connected now than ever. There's video calls and messaging, and we could make sure we fly out to see each other as often as possible."

Milo's expression changed immediately, from one of dejection to one of elation. "Really? You want to give it a go?"

Keira nodded. "Yes! If you do."

Milo was pulling that face that reminded her of a Labrador. It was like all his Viking monuments had come at once.

"I do," he exclaimed. "I don't want this to stop yet. I think we need to at least try."

Keira nodded. She felt as overjoyed as Milo looked. And for the sake of complete honesty, she added, "In a couple of months, we can think about the next step."

Milo reached over, taking her in his arms. He pressed a kiss into her neck. Keira giggled.

"I'm so happy," she heard him say in her ear.

She snuggled in, breathing in his scent, absorbing his warmth. "So am I."

*

The cab dropped them off at a strange new location Keira had not yet been to; a sort of icy wilderness. She looked around her in wonder, feeling like she'd stepped into Narnia.

"Where are we?" she asked. "And what's with all the snow?"

"We're just a little farther north, and a little higher above sea level, so the temperature is low enough for the snow to not melt," Milo explained. "I thought it would be cool to watch a sled race together."

Keira's mouth dropped open. "Awesome!" she exclaimed. Then she shivered. "I just wish I'd worn my red snowsuit! It's freezing."

Milo reached for her, wrapping his arm around her shoulder. Warmth from his body radiated into her.

"Better?" he asked.

Keira nodded.

They trudged together toward the gathered crowds. Most people in the audience were typically tall Swedes, and Keira had to muscle her way forward in order to be able to see. Just as she caught sight of the track, a group of huskies dragging a sled came racing past. She squealed, in shock and delight, and got a faceful of fluffy snow kicked up under their tracks.

She turned back to face Milo, blinking snow from her lashes. He laughed loudly.

More sleds were approaching, ready to pass them, and Keira started to cheer them on, along with the rest of the crowd. It looked like so much fun, and the dogs were gorgeous. Keira loved huskies. She remembered Anita on the boat and the photo she'd shown her of her own husky, then smiled to herself at the memory. It really had been a great trip.

When the final sled passed, Keira turned to Milo, grinning with exhilaration.

"That. Was. AMAZING!" she cried, sounding as unapologetically enthusiastic as Milo often did.

He seemed thrilled she'd enjoyed herself so much. "Good. I hope that means you'll like our next stop too."

"There's more?" she asked.

He nodded. "Yes. I want you to see all my favorite places before you have to fly home."

He took her hand and led her back through the snow. To Keira's surprise their cab was still waiting, ready to take them to their next stop like a chauffeur. Keira couldn't help but think of the Viking minibus with its neon Swedish flag on the side.

They got in the back and sped away. Keira felt her excitement grow. Milo was great at dates, and she couldn't wait to see what he had lined up.

Keira looked out the window, thinking the view seemed familiar. "We're heading back to Stockholm," she said.

"Yes," Milo told her. "There's a really great place in the city I want you to see."

A short while later, the cab pulled up outside the strangest-looking building Keira had ever seen. It was like an enormous golf ball.

"I'm guessing you haven't brought me here for the architecture," Keira commented as they got out the cab.

Milo laughed. "No. Not at all. This is the Ericsson Globe. The world's largest spherical building."

Keira laughed. Milo just couldn't help himself with the facts!

"It's usually a sporting venue," he explained, "but that's not why we're here."

Keira raised an eyebrow. "Why are we here?" she asked.

Milo just winked. He took her hand and together they went inside. It was very noisy, with lots of flashing lights, and Keira felt a little overwhelmed by the juxtaposition of the winter wonderland and the flashing lights of the globe. On their right was a large, metallic, winding staircase. Milo began leading her up it.

It seemed to go up forever. Keira's legs grew more and more tired. Then finally, they emerged into a large glass dome-shaped room. Keira gasped. Now she understood what was happening. This was a viewing tower, and from here she could see the whole of Stockholm.

"Milo," she gushed, walking over to the window and placing her fingertips against it. "It's amazing."

She felt overwhelmed with emotion, looking out at the view of the city that had made such an indelible mark on her soul. She turned, tears glittering in her eyes.

"Thank you for bringing me here," she whispered.

Milo wrapped his arms around her, holding her tightly, swaying her back and forth, and together they looked out at the amazing city that had brought them together.

*

The night wasn't quite over. Milo had one more trick up his sleeve, and that was dinner in a romantic restaurant.

Unlike the other places he taken her before, this one was quite fancy, and the tables were mainly filled with couples. But whereas just a few days ago Keira would have been mortified to turn up at a place like this wearing the same grubby clothes she'd been in all day, now she couldn't care less. With Milo by her side, such petty concerns became irrelevant. Because life with him on her arm was more fun. The colors of the world were brighter. The music louder.

They took a table in a nook, lit only by warm yellow candlelight. Milo looked stunningly handsome in the light that played across his features. He reached out, holding her hands across the table.

"I've had so much fun these past few days," Keira told him. "Your family is wonderful. I'm going to miss them. And you."

She felt her chest heave with emotion.

"I'm going to miss you too," Milo said. "I can't miss your family, though, since I've not met them."

Keira chuckled. Milo always knew just the right level of humor to inject into a situation to take the edge off.

172

"You'll meet them one day," she told him, confident in that fact. But then she remembered Cristiano, how quickly things had moved between them, and how that had ultimately ended things between them. "But not for a while. I want you all to myself for the time being."

The server arrived and took their order. They both decided to go with traditional meatballs. It had been Keira's favorite meal in Sweden, followed in close second by reindeer. But meatballs didn't give her the same sense of guilt she got knowing she was chowing down on Donner or Blitzen.

Their food arrived, as well as a bottle of red wine. Keira realized then how little she'd been drinking on this trip. She was glad for it. Too much alcohol messed with her emotions and made her act out. But now, with things on such even footing with Milo, she knew she was safe to let her hair down a little.

"I can't wait to see my family's faces when I give them their gifts," Keira said, thinking of all the sarcastic things she'd purchased.

"Oh yeah, it's almost Christmas," Milo said. "I'd forgotten."

Keira laughed. "How can you forget Christmas? It's everywhere."

Milo gave her hand a squeeze. "I had other things on my mind."

They drank and ate, getting caught up in conversation, savoring every moment they had together. They were so absorbed with one another, neither noticed that the restaurant was closing around them. The server approached.

"I'm so sorry, but we need to lock up now," he said, looking very apologetic.

Keira couldn't believe it; she'd never been so focused on someone that she'd lost sight of the world around her. But that was the effect Milo had on her.

They stood, suddenly aware of the fact they were the only two people in the restaurant, other than some tired and slightly irritated-looking waitstaff. Keira couldn't help but giggle as they headed out the door arm in arm. Once, she'd have been so embarrassed, but now she couldn't care less. There were so many more important things in life, getting stressed over insignificant things just wasn't worth the effort.

They hailed a cab and climbed into the back seat. Hands pressed tightly together, they began the journey back to the mountainside home of Milo's parents.

One more night, Keira thought, mournfully.

But then she told herself she'd just have to make the best of it. She squeezed Milo's hand tightly, and he squeezed back. There were just a few hours left to enjoy one another's company and they were both going to savor it.

CHAPTER THIRTY ONE

Dawn woke Keira, its gray light creeping across the room toward her. She lay in bed, snuggled into Milo's arms, as consciousness returned. She wanted to stay here forever, in this warm bed, with these strong arms around her. But the time had come to go home. To get back to reality, New York City, and the new condo awaiting her. More than any of her trips before, leaving here would feel like waking from the most wonderful dream. She could already tell that by the time she got back to New York City she'd be wondering if any of it had even been real. From the boat trip to the dog sleds to the Northern Lights and the ice bar, it had been a truly magical experience.

She turned in bed, taking in Milo's face. And of course, the most dreamlike thing of all was him. A perfect guy. Funny. Respectful. Smart. Gorgeous. He was everything she'd ever dreamed of and more. She'd never felt this certain about a man before. There was no insecurity with Milo at all. Even after the short time she'd been with him, she trusted him to be honest with her about everything, and that meant there was no shaky ground beneath her feet, nothing to worry about. He would always be straight with her. It was something she hadn't even realized she'd been craving.

He stirred awake then.

"Oh no," he murmured as it dawned on him what day it was. His arms tightened around her waist.

Keira giggled. "I know." She let out a sigh. "It sucks, huh? We'll just have to remember that it's only temporary. We'll see each other again soon."

He nodded and released her.

Keira got out of bed. The room was very cold and her head a little groggy from last night's wine. She dressed in cozy clothes suitable for a long-haul flight, then paced around packing away the rest of her things into her suitcase.

"I can smell coffee," Milo said as he finished dressing himself. "My family must have gotten up early to say goodbye."

Keira smiled, touched that they'd make the effort for her. She really did love them.

They headed downstairs and into the kitchen. There, Milo's family was gathered. On the kitchen island, next to a mug of coffee, sat a stack of beautifully wrapped gifts.

"What are these?" Keira exclaimed.

"Your Christmas gifts," Yolanta said. "Since we won't be seeing you on the day."

Keira was so touched. She hurried forward, hugging Yolanta, Regina, and Nils in turn.

"Thank you, guys," she gushed. She felt her eyes well up. "I'm really going to miss you!"

Everyone bundled in, hugging her. Keira laughed, feeling loved in the big, warm bundle.

"We'd better go," Milo said then, looking at the clock. "We don't want to miss the flight."

Keira was half expecting him to add in a cheeky "Unless..." But he didn't, and she felt strangely deflated, as if he didn't really mind that she was leaving at all. She wondered for the first time whether in the absence of Christmas's naturally imposed deadline, he'd have even asked her to stay.

An old familiar insecurity returned to her as she turned to his family and gave them each one last farewell hug, and then she and Milo headed outside to the little blue car. Keira slung her case in the trunk before taking her seat next to Milo.

"One more road trip," she announced, her voice melancholy.

"One more road trip," he nodded in affirmation.

Again, there was nothing. No suggestion she should stay. No offer. Keira sunk into the seat as Milo started the car and pulled away from the mountainside house, heading for Stockholm Airport.

She mulled everything over in her mind. It wasn't even that she was certain she'd want to stay if he asked, she was just confused that he hadn't even mentioned it as a possibility, even in his usual jokey way. It made her question everything she thought she knew.

Just as they descended from the mountain and onto the main road, Keira's phone began to ring. She thought it would probably be Mallory asking about flight details so she could panic and obsess over when it was landing and if it had been delayed or whether it had crashed, as she was wont to do, but the call was actually from *Viatorum*. Keira frowned.

"It's my boss," she said. "I'd better take this."

Milo made a gesture as if to say go ahead. She answered the call.

"KEIRA!" Elliot bellowed. "Have I ever told you how AMAZING you are?"

176

Keira had to move the phone from her ear, he was shouting so loud. "Uh, not in so many words…"

"Okay, well, you're AMAZING! That article is the best you've ever written. So insightful. So raw and beautiful. We've put an enticement passage up on the website and readers are loving it! They say it's the best one they've read! Our pre-order sales of the winter issue are going through the roof."

"Great," Keira replied.

As thrilled as she was to know her writing was appreciated, the man beside her meant so much more. And she wasn't going to get that much longer with him.

"I'll speak to you when I'm back in New York," she told Elliot, and she ended the call as abruptly as he usually did with her.

But by the time she'd put her phone away, Keira noticed they were on the final approach to the airport. Her heart leapt suddenly, painfully, and before she even had time to think, tears were streaming down her face.

Milo looked over. "Keira…" he said sadly.

She shook her head, too sad to speak.

Milo reached the parking lot and pulled in, Keira still weeping bitterly.

"I'm so sorry," she murmured. But she wasn't embarrassed about her tears, just sorry that this was the final moment he'd share with her.

Of course, Milo dealt with it perfectly. He took her face in his hands, wiping the tears away with his thumbs. When Keira finally met his eyes, she saw that they were welling up too.

He kissed her, deeply, tenderly, expressing love and affection. Keira could feel it all in that one kiss. Love. True love.

Then he pulled away. She took a deep breath and got out the passenger side. She went around to the back of the car and took her case from the trunk, breathing slowly as she did. Then hand in hand they headed toward the terminal.

"I'll stay with you," Milo told her as they went. "Until you're on the plane. I want to get every last second with you I can."

She smiled at him. "Thank you. You're sweet."

They made it to the terminal and Keira looked around for a departures board. She saw a large one and headed toward it, Milo in tow. And there it was, the flight to take her home.

She turned to Milo. "I guess this is goodbye."

"For now," he said with assurance.

Keira hesitated. They'd talked about this break only being temporary, about wanting to carry on long distance, but Milo's complete reluctance to suggest she stay with him was making her question his genuine intentions. But this was *Milo,* she reminded herself. He was always honest with her; it was one of the qualities she adored in him.

She opened her mouth, about to ask him why, when Milo began to speak, beating her to it.

"Keira, I want you to stay," he blurted. "I know you promised your mother you'd spend Christmas with her, and you have all those gifts you need to take back home, but I think you'd have a great time here and I'm not ready to say goodbye."

His words came out in one huge rush, like he'd actually been worried himself to admit how he felt.

Keira blinked, surprised. It was as if he'd read her mind. All she could think to say was, "Why didn't you ask before?"

Milo shifted uncomfortably. "I didn't ask because I was worried to hear you say no."

His admission took her even more aback. Since when was Milo one to worry about the outcome of his words? He must have been so concerned about her rejecting him he'd gone against all his instincts not to bring it up in the open.

And as the cogs of Keira's mind whirred, she wondered whether he'd been picking up on subliminal cues from her, because now that he'd said it, she herself wasn't sure. Mixed feelings swirled in her head. Keira thought of Mallory, of the promise she'd made her mother to be there for Christmas. She'd never missed Christmas before. It was supposed to be a time for family. But she wondered if perhaps that was what love meant, taking those leaps away from the familiar, moving out of one's comfort zone. Maturing, building one's own life and family, would inevitably mean leaving one's childhood family behind. The thought scared her. But was Milo the right person to make that first, daring step with?

Because what if it didn't go well, and she was in a foreign country, missing home, during the time of the year when family was so important?

Then an even scarier thought struck her. What if it went well? What if it went very well indeed? Then what? What would it mean, if she fell so in love with this guy she wanted him to become part of her family? What would come next? Could there be a future for them?

She'd need to go home to her own country at some point; she and Milo had their own lives on separate sides of the globe, and that wasn't going to change anytime soon. So why risk it? Why let things develop when she knew they had to end?

Keira recalled the previous times when there *had* been a future—a willingness from Shane to have a long-distance relationship between Ireland and New York City. Cristiano's willingness to move his entire life from Italy to be with her. Neither of them had worked out, either.

Even if this relationship appeared to have no way forward, perhaps that was the exact time to go against common sense and leap into it headfirst. To stop pondering the future and enjoy this one moment, this one unique Christmas, a moment that could stay with her forever. Because when she was old, even if she and Milo never saw each other again, she'd be able to look back and remember how brave and bold she'd once been. She thought about life and fate, and the way the universe had brought them together, two strangers in a foreign country, now united in love.

At last, she squeezed Milo's hands. A smile spread across her lips as she uttered the most daring word of her life.

"Yes."

"Yes?" Milo said, his eyebrows rising. "You'll stay?"

Keira's grin grew bigger still, in response to his obvious joy and relief. She nodded vigorously. "Yes. I'll stay!"

Milo swept her into his arms, spinning her on the spot. Keira squealed, feeling free and daring, bold and liberated. She'd found her independence after all, just not in the way she'd been expecting.

Milo set her back on her feet and took her face gently in his hands. He kissed her, pressing soft, tender lips against hers. Keira felt a swirl of pleasure radiating from her stomach, taking over her entire body.

"You're vibrating," Milo said.

Keira frowned. "Huh?"

He laughed. "Your phone. I think."

Keira laughed too, realizing what he meant, and pulled her cell phone out of her pocket. It was an email from Elliot. She could see the subject line in her notification: WHAT ABOUT SWEDISH GUY?

She thought for a second. The old Keira would reply.

Instead, she shut her phone off and powered it down.

She didn't care if the ending of her article was unsatisfactory for Elliot. This was *her* life, *her* relationship, and she wanted to keep parts of it private, to herself, like a secret only she and Milo shared.

"What was that?" Milo asked, wrapping his arm around her shoulder.

"Nothing," Keira said with a nonchalant shrug.

He guided her from the airport, heading away from the departure board that just moments earlier had signaled the end of their time together.

Arm in arm, they headed through the airport, toward the big glass doors.

And toward the next step of their lives together.

LOVE LIKE YOURS
(The Romance Chronicles—Book 5)

"LOVE LIKE THIS creates a world of emotions and turmoil, describing superbly the mind of a young lady (Keira) and her struggles to balance her social life and her career. Sophie Love is a natural storyteller. LOVE LIKE THIS is very well written and edited, and I highly recommend it to the permanent library of all readers that appreciate a romance that can be savored during a weekend."
--Books and Movie Reviews (Roberto Mattos)

LOVE LIKE YOURS (The Romance Chronicles—Book #5) is book #5 in a new, sweet romance series by #1 bestselling author Sophie Love. The series begins with LOVE LIKE THIS (Book #1), a free download!

Keira Swanson, 28, finds herself spending a magical Christmas with new her new boyfriend and his family in Sweden. How will their relationship end?

Keira returns to New York to discover, to her shock, that she has started a new trend in dating that is sweeping across the country— "Scandinavian romance"—and to find herself becoming a celebrity. Even more confusing, her sister gets engaged, and gives Keira constant advice. Overwhelmed, Keira takes solace when Christiano calls, and surprises herself when she agrees to take a week off and meet him on neutral ground: in Greece.

Her magazine is thrilled, and they want this to be her new assignment: can love work the second time around, in a different time and place, if you give it one more chance?

Greece is spectacular, filled with sun, ocean, ruins and romance. It is one of the most beautiful places she has ever been. But nothing can prepare Keira for her encounter with Cristiano—and the surprise that follows on its heels.

A wholesome romantic comedy that is as profound as it is funny, LOVE LIKE YOURS is book #5 in a dazzling new romance series that will make you laugh, cry, and will keep you turning pages late into the night—and will make you fall in love with romance all over again.

Book #6 will be published soon!

"Sophie Love's ability to impart magic to her readers is exquisitely wrought in powerfully evocative phrases and descriptions....[This is] the perfect romance or beach read, with a difference: its enthusiasm and beautiful descriptions offer an unexpected attention to the complexity of not just evolving love, but evolving psyches. It's a delightful recommendation for romance readers looking for a touch more complexity from their romance reads."
--*Midwest Book Review* (Diane Donovan re: *For Now and Forever*)

Sophie Love

#1 bestselling author Sophie Love is author of the romantic comedy series, THE INN AT SUNSET HARBOR, which includes eight books, and which begins with FOR NOW AND FOREVER (THE INN AT SUNSET HARBOR—BOOK 1).

Sophie Love is also the author of the debut romantic comedy series, THE ROMANCE CHRONICLES, which includes 5 books (and counting), and which begins with LOVE LIKE THIS (THE ROMANCE CHRONICLES—BOOK 1).

Sophie would love to hear from you, so please visit www.sophieloveauthor.com to email her, to join the mailing list, to receive free ebooks, to hear the latest news, and to stay in touch!

BOOKS BY SOPHIE LOVE

THE INN AT SUNSET HARBOR
FOR NOW AND FOREVER (Book #1)
FOREVER AND FOR ALWAYS (Book #2)
FOREVER, WITH YOU (Book #3)
IF ONLY FOREVER (Book #4)
FOREVER AND A DAY (Book #5)
FOREVER, PLUS ONE (Book #6)
FOR YOU, FOREVER (Book #7)
CHRISTMAS FOREVER (Book #8)

THE ROMANCE CHRONICLES
LOVE LIKE THIS (Book #1)
LOVE LIKE THAT (Book #2)
LOVE LIKE OURS (Book #3)
LOVE LIKE THEIRS (Book #4)
LOVE LIKE YOURS (Book #5)

Made in the USA
Lexington, KY
08 September 2018